MEDUSA'S CURSE
THE MONSTERS OF GODS
BOOK 1
AF407048
JOSSLYN LEACH

Her crowning glory
writhed & hissed
& stated the air.
Men averted their eyes,
& Medusa grinned.
She knew mortals
could not endure
her rare beauty.

— FROM SILENCE IS
      BEAUTY

Dedicated to Tasha. Girl you now finally have your gothic dream group of eggplants.
*You lucky duck, *wink, wink*.*
All seriousness, thank you for everything you have done. All the confidence you have instored into me, and all the goofy talks. Now enjoy your book, I'll just be over here sitting in the corner drinking my coffee like a creeper.

CONTENT WARNING

Medusa's Curse is an adult read with adult concepts.

All sexual acts are consensual in this book, (except one chapter has a scene where a character is spelled to think another is their true mate and they do have a sexual moment,) other than that it is all consensual.

This book is also a why choose paranormal romance, which means Medusa and other characters are sexually active with others. It also means Medusa will have more than one mate. It is also mixed with a bit of romantic comedy and heap of fantasy.

This book has M/M- so if you don't want to read about men having a relationship or sex with each other than stop here and close the book because they do and I'm not changing it.

The men in Medusa's life are also mated to each other and you will get to experience the love they have for each other and Medusa throughout this story.

It is a multi-point of view, so you will also get to read from not only Medusa's experiences but the men in her life's experiences.

ENTIRELY FICTIONAL.

It is also a twist on Medusa, most of the things I've written do not match with what you have read or studied in ancient Greek mythology, and I meant for it to be that way. I have also used many other Greek gods and inspiration of the monsters in my story, and most will not match up to Greek mythology either.

I also felt the need to add many other mythical creatures into this story; most will not be what you expect of them.

Don't hate my book for it.

Medusa's Curse may not be suitable for all readers. Please look after yourself, first and foremost.

It also has a cliffy ending. Just a heads up for those that hate books with cliffhangers. I'd say sorry but I'm not. It's an amazing ending and gives the story that extra dash of spice.

Loreath Realm Map

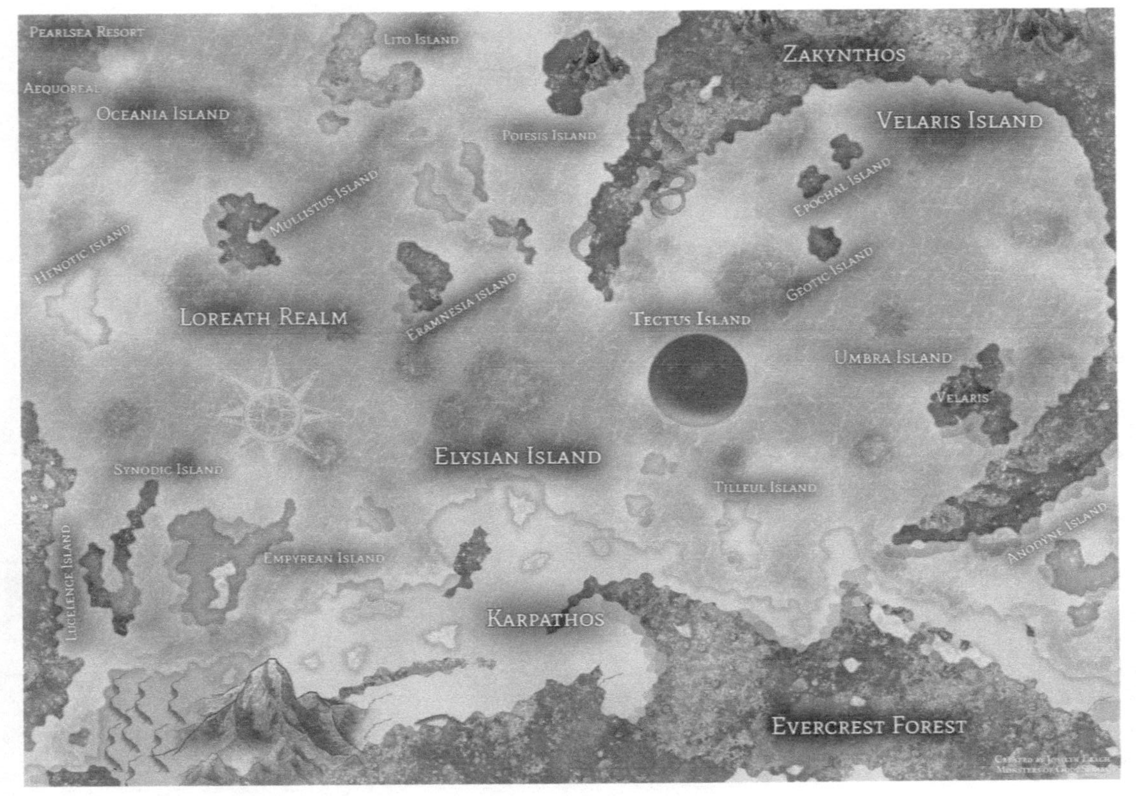

CHAPTER 1
MEDUSA

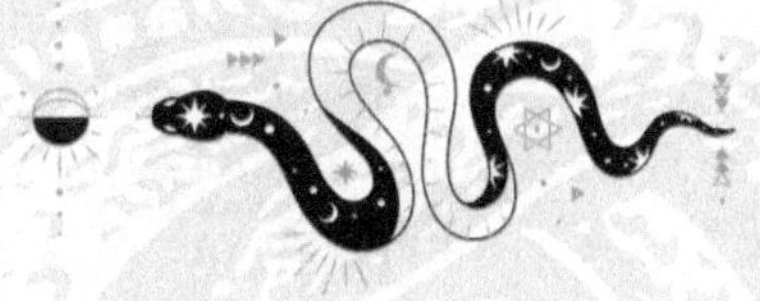

Destiny is such a fickle thing, a single choice or event can alter the fate of so many others, creating a domino effect of different possibilities. At the moment I wanted to scream fuck the possibilities. They couldn't be worse than the stress of being "invited" to attend the Hera's Birthday Celebration has me feeling completely out of sorts. Heading towards my rustic cabin in the woods, hidden amongst the natural flora and fauna, it's one of the few places that brings me peace.

According to the invitation, all gods and goddesses were invited "no matter how small your talents are." That's seriously what the invitation said. Only a prick like Zeus would add something so offensive, compensating much? And yet he is the one who rules over us, the one we look to for guidance and peace. When his Queen, Hera, summoned me to use my gifts to enhance her party, the brief glimpses I caught of him made me feel physically ill. He has a vile aura around him, one that makes me try to spend the least amount of time around him, lest his foul aura spreads like a contagious disease.

When I finally reach my sanctuary, I take a deep breath in. The fresh air clears away the last of my fear from helping Hera get her gardens ready for tonight. My spirits lifting even more the moment I spot my familiar and his mate waiting for me on the steps of my small rustic cabin.

The place isn't huge, but it is mine. Helping creatures surrounded by nature gives me the peace my soul craves, for this reason, I moved my sanctuary to Evercrest Forest.

Evercrest Forest is uniquely one of a kind. No one really knows where this magically enchanted forest ends, and many have gotten lost trying to navigate through the different zones of the forest. Each zone is unique and different, the forest magic alive, and allowing only certain Gods and Goddesses through.

The area I was gifted with is an enthralling copse of towering ancient and sentient trees surrounding my land, their smooth gray trunks covered in delicate lace-like moss.

Beams of sunlight peek through the canopy of leaves above. Once the sun sets, tiny glowing dots of gold, blue and purple light up my forest. These tiny dots firelightsects, called firepix, fly around the forest illuminating and casting the forest in beautiful colors. While the ground is blanketed in lush flora, aromatic flowers, and curly ferns. The ground is blanketed in lush flora, aromatic flowers, and curly ferns.

Most gods or goddesses with creature or nature gifts usually find a place within the forest to build a home that fits them best. There is even a special place for the God Guardian creatures.

The true gem of my forest is the Crystal Lake down a small path from my home. At the edge of the water is a large wooden deck Atticus helped me build.

The lake is so full of life, colorful creatures of all shapes and sizes swim through the clear waters. Fine white sand blankets the lake floor with an array of beautiful stones and coral. This lake is teeming with all forms of life from creature to plant, all of which respond to my magic. My favorite pastime is to wake up and take tea down by the water and watch the breathtaking show the fish put on.

"Good morning, Loki and Jezebel," I say to my tortoise familiar and his mate as I scratch the top of their heads before opening the door.

I leave it open so that Loki and Jezebel can come inside for breakfast. Heading directly into the kitchen to grab the fruits, vegetables, and lotus flowers they both love.

"Good morning, Medusa." I hear a deep-timbre voice say behind me.

"Fuck!" I scream, as my soul tries to jump from my body. Automatically I turn, throwing the apple in my hand at the intruder.

Catching the apple inches from his face Atticus tsks, "Medusa stop throwing Loki's breakfast, it isn't nice."

"Then stop sneaking into people's homes and scaring them. Be thankful it wasn't a knife this time." I reply, reminding him of the one time I did throw a knife.

Standing up from the couch, he walks over towards me, "both my hand and I are thankful it wasn't." He replies with a smirk handing me back the apple.

I take it from him, our fingers brushing, our close contact sending a pleasant buzzing sensation through my body, I wonder briefly if our simple touch affects him the same way. We both stare down at our touching hands. Before my eyes can meet his too intense stare, Atticus leans in closer, "Medusa I- " and before he gets a word out to finish his sentence Atticus is knocked down on the ground and I can hear Loki hissing and croaking unhappily at him.

"He said it's rude not to say hi, and he thinks you should do penance for also giving me a fright," I tell Atticus.

Turning my back to him, I start slicing up the fruit before he can get up off the ground and witness the pink staining my cheeks. For a moment there, I thought he was going to kiss me. A kiss I've only dreamed about. Sadly, he was claimed by Circe before I could muster up enough courage to tell Atticus my true feelings. By the time I was ready to declare my feelings, Circe had him attached firmly to her side. Suddenly, I became his third wheel best friend.

It got to the point where I couldn't even stand to be around them. It just ate at my heart to see the man I was utterly in love with, fall for another.

"I'm sorry Loki, I didn't mean to scare Medusa, and I definitely did not realize you were here as well, or I would have come and said hi to you and Jezebel." Atticus says.

A big smile graces my lips while listening to him chat with my familiar who is threatening his life if he ever scares me again. And of course, I pass along Loki's sweet sentiments. Adding a few finishing touches to their plates I finally have their food ready for them. Bringing their plates over and sitting next to my best friend on the floor watching them both eat.

"So where is Circe?" I ask softly, trying to act like I'm genuinely curious where the evil witch of the west isles is since she isn't attached to his arm at the moment. She's probably finding some new way to shove their relationship in my face, adding extra lemon juice and salt to the injury for the hell of it.

Leaning back on his arms he says, "I broke up with her."

Turning my head so fast I swear I just gave myself whiplash, I blurt out," you broke up with her?"

He smiles softly at me, "we're not good for each other.

We didn't fit together, the way I feel that two souls should." Grabbing my hand in his, it makes my heart start to thunder in my chest. Any faster, and we'd be seeing it burst from my body. "She wasn't the one my soul yearned for, leaving me restless and aching for her."

"And who is?"

"You." he states simply, like it should be obvious, like he didn't completely blow my world open. Speechless, my mind is utterly useless. I can't speak or move. While I'm still taking in what he just confessed to me. By some miracle, I finally find my voice.

"Me?" I say pointing at myself while looking desperately around the room for someone else he could be talking to. Loki and Jezebel are the only other occupants of the room, and it still takes another few seconds for the reality of his statement to seep in.

Not my brightest moment.

A husky chuckle catches my attention. "Yes you, Medusa. You are the only Goddess for me. Will you forgive me for being so blind and not seeing what you are to me before this?" He sounds nervous and unsure of himself, and it makes me sad to think that he's been as blind to my love as I have his. "If not, I understand why you can't. I mean who would, after me and... never mind. I'll just go." Atticus starts to get up. "My mom also wanted you at her house by five to get ready for Hera's Birth Celebration."

I smile at the flustered God before me, pressing my lips gently to his. He only seems surprised for a moment before taking control of the kiss. Deepening it as his lips press against mine with an urgency and passion that I'd never thought I'd receive. His tongue runs across the seam of my lips as if asking for permission to enter. With new bravado, I draw his tongue into my mouth. Needing no more permission, Atticus takes hungry possession of my mouth, his hands lifting me till I straddle his lap. I moan into his mouth as his hard length grinds into me and his wicked mouth devours my every thought as the world is fading around us.

CHAPTER 2
ATTICUS

Feeling Medusa's soft lips pull from mine I growl and nip at her lips causing a breathy moan to escape. If I could devour that sound I would, and if we had the time, I'd devour her.

Medusa has no idea what she means to me. How just the smell of her shampoo lingering in the bathroom after her shower calls to me. Anything to do with this goddess calls to me in ways no other has before. It always has, even if it's taken me a while to realize it. I thank the fates endlessly for every moment we have shared. That my feelings for this goddess, who I've known my whole life, became clear before I lost her forever.

Tonight, at Hera's birthday celebration, I will show the other gods and goddesses just what she means to me by claiming her like I should have done years ago as my true mate. My other half. Nothing and no one will keep us apart again.

"So, what are our chances of us skipping out tonight on the ball? We could make dragon bread and maybe some s'mores for dessert?" Medusa asks, still straddling my lap.

Damn, she is so adorable, I want to cave in. Give her everything her heart desires, but I can't.

I nuzzle my face into the space between her neck and shoulder.

"You know we can't," I tell her. I can sense her disappointment.

"Do we have time to stop by The Magical Bean and grab a coffee?"

"Anything for you, my love." I reply, kissing her neck before pulling away reluctantly, and lifting Medusa off me. I stand up before holding out a hand to help Medusa up. We make our way out to the field just to the side of her house where a small shed sits.

"Are you flying or riding?" Medusa asks.

"Riding," I say just as Medusa turns and lets out a whistle.

Most gods don't use transportation, instead, they fly using their wings. Medusa ... well let's just say, being the Goddess of Nature and Creatures has a downfall. Or at least that's what Medusa always says about her wings. When in reality they are an exquisite sight to behold, her stunningly beautiful wings made of vines dotted with purple dahlia pompon flowers that forever keep her grounded.

On most days, Medusa usually walks or rides on the back of her Aequilla. Aequilla are very rare creatures with a horse-like body and a sharp beak on the end of their muzzle. They have long powerful lizard-like tails with tufts of fur lining down their spine, their body covered in a soft fur like horses. They have incredible strength and speed. If they were able to be captured, I have no doubt they would be used for racing, thankfully Zeus has never been game enough to try it. There is a wild herd that lives near Medusa's home and my lovely mate befriended them.

She is one of the only goddesses they allow near them, aside from myself and mother. But I think that is only because Medusa told them we are her family and would never harm them. One, in particular, Lulu, a light pink with a fuchsia mane, is extremely fond of Medusa. If she didn't already have Loki for a familiar, I'd think that Aequilla was made for her.

Of all of the creatures of this land, Aequilla are the most beautiful and deadly, not even the strongest of gods mess with them. The beauty of these animals is deceiving, their nature holding a darker side to them, they have the power to suck your soul and cast it out straight to the underworld. For this reason, it is rumored that they were originally from the underworld. Apparently, Hera had fallen in love with their look and demanded Hades give her them.

Lulu and a midnight blue Aequilla named Nerate, come running out of the forest heading straight for Medusa. Ready as always, she is holding out two sugar cubes one in each hand for the creatures.

"Lulu and Nerate said they'd take us and are willing to make the coffee detour." Medusa tells me as Lulu nuzzles her.

"Perfect," I say before heading into the small shed to grab the reins for the Aequilla. When I come out, I hand Medusa the pink leather reins and special harness for holding coffee cups in, I had it made especially for Medusa and even had it magically spelled so no coffee would spill out no matter how bumpy the ride got. After she starts getting her reins put on Lulu I stroll over to where Nerate stands waiting.

"Hey Nerate, are you ready to show these girls how fast

we can be?" I ask him, sliding the bridle onto his head. He paws at the ground twice which is his way of telling me yes.

"He said you better hope you can stay on this time."

"It was one time, and I didn't see the low-hanging branch. To be honest I think you asked the tree to make that branch hang lower."

"Whatever makes you sleep better." Medusa replies as Lulu lowers to the ground for her to climb her back.

I climb onto Nerates' back and soon they are both taking off, racing through the forest. Their speed is matched as we weave in and out. I look over to see Medusa with her eyes closed and arms wide, branches and plants moving away from her, never more than a leaf or a petal caressing her fingertips. She looks at peace while riding on the back of her Aequilla friend. Soon we start getting closer to town and both Lulu and Nerate slow their speeds down. And Medusa's demeanor goes from happy and free to guarded.

"So how many gods do you think you will have to coax Mixa to spit back out tonight?" I ask her as I wiggle my brows, causing her to laugh. Every time there is a celebration, its owner always brings Mixa, a five-headed serpent who is as mischievous as they come. Each head has its own personality and temperament, apparently, the trick is to treat each head as an individual according to Medusa. At any rate, she's the only one who can walk away unscathed, so I'll just have to take her word for it.

"I'd say about ten," Medusa replies with a giggle.

"I bet you he eats closer to fourteen, you know his owner most likely trapped him inside all day, as a way to try to keep Mixa from running off." I say just as we reach The Magical Bean.

"Damn, you're probably right," she replies.

Knowing Medusa, she is probably planning out how she

is going to deal with the snake tonight. I know that is at least one creature she will help, mostly because his incompetent owner will be begging her to help him. We slide off the backs of our Aequillas who head back to the forest and will wait till Medusa calls for them.

Once inside we place our orders and move off to the side as we wait.

"Did my mom show you the stola she bought for you to wear tonight?" I ask knowing the answer.

My mother took me with her to pick up the stola she had ordered for Medusa. Her reasoning for getting that stola was that she had a good feeling about Medusa's future.

Sometimes, I swear she has more powers than she lets on. Her feelings are never wrong, but she is never clear about them, either. Just a hint here and there or a brief thought, like; she "has a good feeling", or "don't go to the lake, it's a bad day for that."

Shaking her head, no, "She has refused to show me, only telling me that I'm going to love it."

"Oh, you will." I answer as I pull her hand into mine, lifting it up and pressing my lips against the back.

CHAPTER 3
MEDUSA

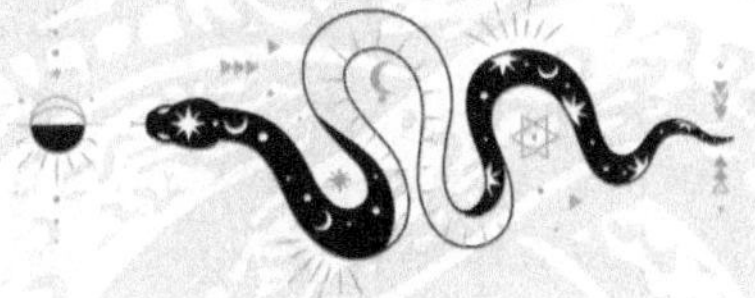

The barista calls out our names and we rush out of the cafe heading to Atticus' mother's home.

Sumerian took me in after my mother died. Her death is still a confusing mystery to me. Aside from a father I had never met, I didn't have any other family that I knew of. All I know is my mother said he made her feel something she never felt before, a spark in her soul that called for him. Sumerian took me in as an infant, all of the stories surrounding my mother are all secondhand memories, I don't even know if my father knows of my existence.

As we ride up the stone path, I can see Sumerian is standing on the porch waiting for us.

"Is it too late for me to hide in the forest and miss the celebration?" I ask Atticus as I slump down on my Aequilla's back trying to hide from Suma's gaze as we come to a stop in the front garden.

I mean if I can't see her, she can't see me, right? I swear that's a thing.

A sudden throat-clearing next to me makes my heart

leap from my chest, my balance becoming a separate entity and fleeing, as my clumsy self nearly slips off Lulu my scream echoing the surrounding area. Thankfully, I wasn't holding my coffee, or it would be all over me. I briefly look over at Atticus and find him slumped over Nerates' back laughing. I glare at him before facing Sumerian who is standing next to me smiling suppressing a laugh.

Unlike the ogre next to me, Summerian is a sweet gentle goddess with long dark blue hair, dark as night. My favorite feature has to be her eyes. When close up, they reflect the starry night sky. Glowing constellations burning bright, reflecting her inner light within when she has her visions. Okay, so Atticus isn't an ogre. He's very much the opposite, when standing next to each other, both mother and son radiate similar energies and could be confused as brother and sister since we are ageless entities.

Though where Sumerian's beauty reflects the night sky Atticus is like the sun with a strong jaw, eyes that glimmer gold and silver depending on his mood, deep golden hair shaved on the sides and longer on the top that makes my fingers itch to run through, he really embodies the classic "god look" and the muscles to back it.

"Medusa, are you hungry, you have a little drool dripping down your chin?" Atticus says as he wipes the side of my chin.

"I'm fine," I say, embarrassed turning away to discreetly wipe my own face. Grabbing my drink and the extra one for Sumerian before sliding off Lulu's back. Setting the drinks down I quickly undo the reins and satchel before grabbing the delectable nectar and turning to face Suma.

"So, this is what took you both so long to return home?" Sumerian says with a knowing smirk.

"You know me mother, I couldn't say no when Medusa

asked to grab coffee before you wrestled her into formal wear," Atticus says as he throws his arm around my shoulders. Glaring up at him shrugging his arm off and handing Sumerian her coffee.

"I know what you mean, son. Come Medusa, let's get you ready for a night that is bound to be filled with new adventures." She says with a knowing wink before she turns and heads back towards the house, not looking back to see if I'm even following.

Atticus throws his arm back over my shoulder, "Don't worry Medusa, I promise I'll keep everyone from asking you questions about their pets tonight. It will be a night to remember." He promises before kissing the top of my head softly as we step inside the house. I know he will attempt to keep his word on trying to keep all the gods from me, but we both know that it might be a futile effort. I mean we already placed bets on Mixa, and he is not the only dangerous creature that will be there tonight.

Heading into my bedroom where Sumerian is already waiting for me, she has set up the vanity with all the makeup and items she will use to doll me up.

"Go take a quick shower Medusa, then we will get started on your hair and make-up," she tells me before walking over to my bookcase, grabbing one of the books on the shelves, and making herself at home on the window seat. I don't hesitate, making my way into my bathroom to shower.

I can't help but laugh while taking in my hair in the mirror. My thick wavy green locks have held on to pieces of sticks and leaves from my latest romp in the forest. While I love my hair, I hate how it seems to have a mind of its own. I do try to keep it a certain length, certain strong emotions cause it to grow at a rapid rate. When Atticus and Circe started dating, I probably spent a week in hiding learning to meditate, so I could better control my emotions. I'm pretty sure that's the reason all the birds had bits of my hair lining their nests.

With a sigh I turn the water on, letting it warm up while I get to work, removing as much of the debris from my hair before stripping and stepping into the shower's warm embrace. I finally find the strength to leave the shower when the water starts to cool, drying off and lathering up my skin.

"Medusa you put on any more layers of lotion, and you'll slide right out of your dress tonight." Sumerian says from outside the bathroom.

Muttering to myself while I wrap up in my robe, spotting Sumerian tucking away one of my old smutty books. With a snicker, she says "while I work my magic on your hair and make-up, I want your opinion on if you think it's possible the female lead in that story was truly hydrated enough to take on that many men for hours at a time without a water break?"

"Sweet underworld! Swallow me now." I say as my eyes bounce around the room looking for the quickest way out.

"Now, now Medusa, as the daughter of my heart it is my duty to educate you on the importance of hydration and lubrication, why, back in my day, I would spend hours with Atticus' father, he used to do this thing with his hips while his best friend held me up..."

"Suma," I beg, hearing about the closest thing you have to a mother talking about her sex life... let's just say I hope bringing up the childhood name I gave her will help me get out of this conversation.

"You spend way too much time alone in the woods, this celebration has big things in store for you," she smiles down at me slyly. I sit down and instantly Suma gets to work, facing me away from the mirror for a surprise reveal.

"I don't know if anyone could truly go hours without some kind of break." I answer honestly as I feel my cheeks grow warm.

I hear Suma snicker, "if you turn any redder your beautiful face is going to attract bugs wanting to pollinate it as they think it's a new flower."

I sit up straighter, "So Suma what is your opinion on proper hydration." I ask, smiling when I hear Summerian start choking on air.

Score one for Medusa.

My win is short lived when Suma tells me about how she not only was able to stay properly hydrated but also how she handled more than one man. By the end I was well educated on Suma's sexcapades. And honestly, I now needed a potion to erase all said images from my mind.

"I need you to stand up but keep your eyes closed." Suma says as she heads towards my closet.

"How on earth am I going to get dressed with my eyes closed." I grumble as I stand with my back facing the mirror.

"I've got you Medusa, just close those pretty purple eyes of yours and trust me." Suma tells me. With a few choices mumbles I do as she says, closing my eyes while I wait for further instructions.

"Alright Medusa, hold onto my shoulder." Suma instructs me as she guides my hand to her shoulder to help me keep my balance before I step into the stola. Suma glides the silky material up my body to my hips. "Keep your eyes shut but remove your robe for me so I finish getting you dressed." Suma tells me, of course I oblige and soon she has pulled up the dress. I feel her latch something on my wrist.

"You can look now." Suma whispers before I hear the door to my room close.

Turning to face the full-length mirror in the room for the first time. I'm speechless, in front of me stands a goddess, one whose beauty is exotic and wild. The dark purple gem stola I wear accentuates my eyes and frames my body with silky material gathered at the top of my right shoulder with a golden cap sleeve. A lilac sleeve flows down my arm with a delicate golden string of chains forming a decorative cuff around my wrist. Sumerian left my hair down to cascade around in green vine like curls, with flowers and gems woven throughout it.

"Now you truly look like the goddess of nature," Sumerian says as she re-enters my room and comes to stand next to me. Her deep blue stola is decorated with a smattering of gems that look like the stars have been woven into the seams of the fabric.

"Only because you are a miracle worker," I reply in awe.

"I only helped enhance your inner beauty. Hopefully, soon you will see how much it shines out for the world to see." She whispers to me just as Atticus walks into my room. Pausing his eyes take me in before they reach my own, our gazes meeting in a silent standoff. My heartbeat races as a mixture of emotions play across his face, the longing, adoration, and desire speaking to me better than words ever could.

"Is the carriage here yet?" Sumerian asks, dragging his attention away from me.

I smile letting my eyes rake up his body while his attention is distracted. Taking in the sight of the stunning golden god that stands before me in a white toga with delicate golden accents.

I am pretty sure my brain has short circuited; I've lost control of the modest goddess I try to be as my eyes soak in the sight of Atticus' scarcely covered body. While Atticus and I have grown up together and been with each other through our awkward phases, there is something about his bared nipple that is just taking me places. By the time I have gained enough to school my expression I know I've been caught. His cocky smile says it all.

"Don't you dare say it, Medusa. You know this is the official clothes for the Gods."

I suppress the smile that is threatening to escape my innocent expression, "Atticus, you know I would never begrudge you that blissful feeling of relief one gets when you get a nice breeze up your undercarriage." I say passing him, capturing his eyes as I flick said nipple, rushing to the front door.

"I told you that in confidence Dusa!!"

Atticus chases after me causing squeals of laughter to ring out in the air as I push my shorter legs to move faster than his much longer ones. Stopping only when his hand latches onto my wrist pulling me back and twisting me in his arms so that my hands lay flush against his chest.

"Medusa?"

"Yes?" I ask.

"Can I keep you?" He asks as he brushes a stray hair behind my ear. I smile at his words while my butterflies flutter in my stomach. The words he once asked me when we were kids make this moment even more magical.

"Forever, until the sun needs you in the sky." I say responding to him as I did all those years ago when we were young and free.

CHAPTER 4
MEDUSA

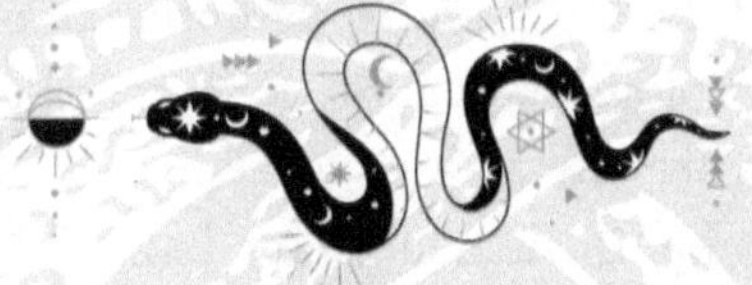

The moment Zeus and Hera's home comes into view a sense of dread starts to suck away all of the warm, happy feelings I had prior. It is grand in every way; flowers of every species are planted in her gardens. I should know, she called me to help make them all vibrant a few days before the party. The gardens are her pride and joy, and I don't blame her, colorful stained-glass lanterns dispersed through the mixture of flowers and vines create an elegant backdrop.

All while Hera's peacocks wander the yard, their tails of color fluttering behind them, filling spaces with their beauty. The birds are all uniquely beautiful, some like the ones the humans are familiar with, and others are the colors of sunsets, sunrises, and the night sky. Rumor is, that some of the peacocks are Zeus's old lovers that Hera cursed to be the beautiful birds so that her mate could never fuck another one of them again.

Working with some of these birds I can tell the rumors are true. I sometimes believe that the Gods and Goddesses forget about my ability to communicate with creatures when I help them with their gardens. So far, in speaking with the birds, I know that Zeus and Hera fight at least twice a day minimum, if Hera is feeling extra petty, they'll fight on the terrace so she can use the birds as ammo with his infidelities. After a long yelling match, they'll make up in full view of the birds, and apparently, Zeus prefers doggy style so he can blow kisses at his audience of ex-lovers, while thrusting into his wife.

Goddess, he is such a smug bastard. With nothing better to do, the magical birds have started taking bets on how long he'll last, if they'll catch him later that night sneaking out, and if he'll bring the dumb unsuspecting goddess back. I end up finding out more than I bargain for. Apparently, because I've registered as a goddess of low magical status, it hasn't registered that I technically could have all sorts of eyes and ears within all of the houses. They are all quite lucky I choose to use my powers for good.

"Are you both ready?" Sumerian asks Atticus and I.

I nod, stepping out of our carriage and making our way up the path heading towards the house. My heart is pounding as fast as a hummingbird's wings with every step that brings us that much closer to the ballroom. Other Gods linger around the front gardens socializing with each other before they head inside. Sumerian leads the way while Atticus walks next to me, our fingers brushing as he moves closer to my side.

Sumerian suddenly moves to my other side as we turn left, heading towards the ballroom. Something in the air feels off, like a residue of old magic trying to cling to me, but hitting a barrier, repelling it away. I don't even think either of them knows but it's like they can feel it as well and want to protect me from whatever the fates have in store for me tonight. I can only hope it is a good thing, and not something that ends in my death. Of course, that only means someone would have had to smuggle in one of the forbidden weapons into the God of Gods' home.

These weapons are forged in the hottest of fires and cooled in the Styx River, the weapon is the only thing that effectively ends a god and while there is a general idea at how they are made, the enchantments placed on these are a closely guarded secret. Only one of the forbidden weapons can ensure a true death, otherwise, we float around till our essence comes back together but that can take anywhere from a few weeks to a few months, occasionally centuries.

Grabbing my hand, my childhood best friend sends all the negative feelings I have about this night out the door. I smile up at him as he squeezes my hand, as we keep walking. I can now see the giant gold doors that have large rubies and pearls encrusted into a bolt of lightning. Every step we take brings us closer till we finally stand before them. Atticus lets go of my hand but steps in even closer to my side. The doors swing open splitting Zeus's symbol, stepping forward we now stand up on the top of a grand staircase.

Magar, the god of sound, steps up to his side, "Atticus, the God of the Sun and Moon, Sumerian the Goddess of the Moon and Venus, and Medusa the Goddess of Nature and Creatures." His voice echoes across the room the size of the coliseums the gladiators used to fight in. At once, all the Gods and Goddesses turn their gazes to us as we walk down the stairs.

"Head up high Medusa, let them see the light shine from within you, my darling girl." Suma whispers to me.

I do as she says, a few gasps fill the air, but I don't dare move to see what has caused this, scared I'd lose the confidence that I have suddenly gained in this moment. In the presence of so many powerful beings, showing weakness is something no god or goddess can afford to do. Even when I see Circe and her gang staring daggers in my direction, I pretend to be confident and powerful just like everyone else. Circe smirks as she whispers to her friends and then in an instant, they disappear from sight. Once we reach the ballroom floor, the room returns to the earlier sounds of talking, glasses clinking, and the music playing in the background.

"Come dance with me, Medusa," Atticus says as he grabs my hand and drags me to the dance floor swiping two gold chalices from a passing server.

I look back over my shoulder and see Sumerian intercept the usual flock of Gods and Goddesses that normally come up to me and waste my night with their questions. Handing me the chalice with a wink, Atticus says "let's make tonight a night to remember."

Clinking my glass to his, I counter, "to getting drunk and watching a giant snake eat gods." Taking a healthy gulp of liquid courage and draining the beautiful glass dry.

Once I've finished off the glass, Atticus took my chalice, placing it with his own on a passing serving tray. I smile at Atticus, for the first time in my life it feels like I'm on the right path. One that I never saw coming, only dreamt about and wished on a star or two for.

"What are you thinking about Medusa?" Atticus asks, pulling me into his arms.

Wrapping my arms around his neck, I answer him truthfully. "How lucky I am now that I can call you mine."

"I believe I'm the lucky one." He responds as we start swaying to the beat. I don't argue but I'm most definitely thanking the fates.

CHAPTER 5
CIRCE

"Yes, harder my king!" I scream out as the King of Gods fucks me. Pounding himself deep into my wet heat with such ferocity it might break me. He grabs me by the throat pulling me back against him. I love it when he gets so rough, it feels like I'm being split in two with equal parts agony and pleasure.

"Only if my good girl does exactly what we agreed upon. Send out the curse for Medusa."

"I will, my King. I'd do anything for you." I pant out. He leans down, smashing his lips to mine in a punishing kiss. Nipping my lips before releasing my throat and fucking me harder than he ever has. I will be feeling his marks for days. His fingers dig into my hips, I know when he is done with me, bruises will mar my skin. With one last pump of his hips Zeus comes and I follow like a good girl.

"Thank you, my King."

He pulls me to my feet. "It's always a pleasure to have these moments with you Circe. Now run along. You and your friends have some magic to make."

I nod my head quickly, dressing before I head out the

door. The twins holding the power of discord and wrath, Atte and Eris, have become very useful to me. If they hadn't been obedient and powerful in their own right, I would have discarded them ages ago. Stepping out of the room and closing the door I see the twins right where I left them keeping watch.

Grabbing Atte's chin between my fingers I press my lips to hers pushing her against the door. Sliding my tongue into her mouth I grab the back of her head firmly, causing her to gasp out. I feel Eris step up close behind me.

"We need you," she says, her voice husky with need. Pulling my mouth away from Atte's I turn my gaze to Eris.

"Is that how you speak to your queen? Prove to me how much you need me." I say sitting in the chair across the hall, leaning back, "stop talking and show your mistress what you want." I say leaning my head back and trailing my hand down my breasts continuing down and lifting the layers of my stola high enough to bare myself to them. I smile seductively as I watch them stalk closer to me, my breath hitching when I spot Zeus watching in the doorway.

His dick in his hand, I don't take my eyes off of him as I magically undress the twins just as Eris reaches me, dropping to her knees alternating between kissing and licking up my thighs, moaning at the sight of me completely spread and dripping from my recent rendezvous with the king. Tasting our combined release, Eris pulls my legs over her shoulder and plunges her tongue in deep. Atte then surprises me as she comes up behind me biting down on my neck and fondling my large breasts. They both work in sync as they bring me closer and closer to my release. Zeus matches their pace as I lace my hand in Eris's lavender hair and ride her face.

"I'm almost there Eris," I whimper, and I move my hips faster looking longingly at Zeus.

One day soon this will be our life, sex, magic, and power. With that last thought, I come hard, my juices coating Eris's face. Before I can move, Zeus is there pressing his dick into my mouth and I suck down his hot thick rope of cum, biting down a little to remind him that he is mine.

"Good girl." he purrs down at me.

My magic ruffles at his praise, "You three better go now before it is too late." Zeus says, leaning down and pressing his lips to mine. "I'll see you later, my soon-to-be queen." He mumbles against my lips before turning and strutting away. I redress myself and magically clean up Eris and Atte before we make our way out to the gardens circling back into the ballroom scoping out the place before I find our target.

"You both know what to do. Make sure every drop gets into her glass." I tell them as I hand them each a vial containing the perfect cocktail to turn Medusa into the only thing that allows Zeus and I to sacrifice her for our cause. Eris and Atte disappear from my side. I grab a glass off a servers' tray as I walk past.

"Gods and Goddess, I'd like to make a toast to my beautiful wife on her special day," Zeus starts off his toast. Tuning out his speech I continue weaving my way through the crowd, once I'm close enough to Medusa and Atticus I turn to face the front pretending I actually give a shit about whatever bullshit Zeus is spouting on about Hera. Slowly I back up until I've knocked Medusa back.

Turning back around, "Oh no I'm sorry I didn't see you there." I say, feigning surprise. Offering her a hand to help her stand back up noticing that I knocked her drink out of her hand. Eri's is a step ahead of me as her and Atte have another drink ready for the nature goddess.

"It's okay Circe, I know you didn't see us behind you." Medusa answers back. Could she be any more pathetic? Really?

"Here is your drink," Atte says as she hands Medusa back the drink.

"Thanks," Medusa replies as we start walking away. Reaching the back corner of the ballroom where the doors lead to a wide-open maze, we stop just before we lose sight of her, the crowded ballroom packed to the brim.

"To Hera," Zeus shouts as he raises his glass.

"To Hera," we all shout, copying his movements before we all drink. Smiling to myself as Medusa downs every last drop of her glass.

It only takes us a moment to reach the center of the maze in the garden, "Thank the shadows, she sheds like a dog," I say, smirking as I place a strand of her dull green hair in the center of the pentagram while Eris and Atte' light the candles.

Taking a deep breath in letting it out tilting my head back, my face looking up at the sky. I smile, seeing the moon in the perfect position above us. The shadows must be on my side tonight, as the night sky is perfectly clear, revealing a full moon.

"Ready?" I ask my lovers and faithful servants, taking my place at the top of the pentagram while they each move to a different point of the star, forming a triangle.

"Always," they answer together, as one.

"With all our heart and might we hex Medusa, till the end of time, sealing her embodiment from the form of a goddess to a monster." taking the dagger hidden in a holder on my thigh, I slice Eris's hand.

She turns it over and lets her blood drip onto Medusa's hair.

"I curse you Medusa, with the serpent's hair," Eris says with a hiss.

I then slice Atte's hand, and she smirks at me as she lets her blood fall on top of Eris's. "I curse you Medusa, with a serpent's tail."

Finally, I cut my own palm and let my blood trickle onto her hair. "I curse you Medusa, to become a monster of nightmares."

"So, mote it be," we finish together.

Smiling as we watch Medusa's hair, and the mixture of our offerings catch flame I wrap an arm around Atte's waist while grasping Eris's hand in my own.

"Let's get back to the ball." I say turning my back to our burning offering and strolling towards the ballroom knowing that the hair will have become ash by the time we've reached the doors.

CHAPTER 6

MEDUSA

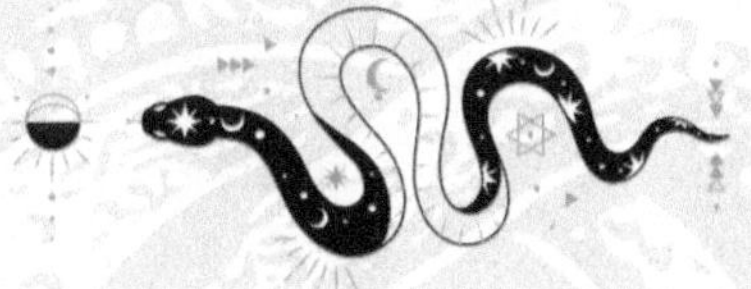

Hera's party was more fun than I had expected it to be. Atticus kept his word by keeping the crazy pet owners away. Looking up at him I can't help but smile, our bodies swaying to the beat. Breathing in his scent of honey and sunshine, calls to my soul. I step in even closer, barely an inch of space keeps our bodies from fully touching. Atticus looks down at me like I'm the only woman in the world causing butterflies to erupt in my stomach.

It is almost laughable at the change in events that have occurred today. All starting with the man swaying with me to the music, my best friend, and the one my heart sings for, my golden god.

"Medusa, there is something I've been wanting to ask you," he says, pulling me from my thoughts.

I smile up at him, "And wh-." I don't even get the chance to finish as I crumble to the ground, my drink falling from my hands, hitting the floor, shattering. I clutch my arms around my stomach as my body instantly feels like it's burning me from the inside out, burning its way out of me. I try to warn Atticus of the inferno trying to escape me. As a scream builds in my throat, but it can't seem to escape as my back arches and my nails dig into the tiles.

"Medusa!" I hear him shout, but I can't answer as the pain is growing worse.

I can feel the dam break. I have never been more thankful, the acid-like burns are starting to fizzle out. Closing my eyes as a scream finally rips past my lips I feel for Atticus, his arms have wrapped around me tightly. Rubbing up and down patterns on my back in his attempt to soothe and take this pain away. Opening my eyes, I can see his mouth moving, but I can't seem to hear his words. The last of the pain is starting to edge out, slowly darkening the corners of my vision, before darkness slowly closes in on me. I try to reach for his face, hopefully showing him that I am starting to feel better.

Until I see Circe step up next to Atticus, her hand on his shoulder as if she was offering support, smirking down at me. The darkness chooses that moment to close in.

The next time I stir I can hear screaming, the words "Monster!" Ring through the air.

Atticus is standing in front of me blocking the crowded group of gods attempting to surround us. Sumerian is sitting with my head in her lap, her hands on either side of my temples. Her lips are moving, but I can't seem to catch the words leaving her mouth as tears fall down her face.

Waves of darkness attempt to pull me under again, only this time the edges around my vision are fuzzy and dark while I try to focus. Everything feels hazy alternating between slow and fast motion.

My eyes fly open as I hear Atticus scream my name, just as the sound of flesh hitting flesh is heard in the background. I'm being carried, I still can't see clearly. I wiggle trying to escape. I need to help Atticus. My effort is futile. I can't move. My body is frozen.

"Atticus" I shout catching the scent of storm and fire surrounding me. It becomes too much, and the feeling I get around Zeus hits me tenfold as my vision finally clears. Everything and everyone surrounding us seems frozen. Everyone but Zeus and I.

With a sinister smile on his face, he leans down and whispers next to my ear. "Let the fates have mercy on you, and pray the ocean takes you fast, because when I find you Medusa you will be mine." Is all he says taking a playful nip of my ear, before tossing me mercilessly off the cliff into the raging ocean below.

Free falling to the depths below, descending into the darkness as the water closes in on me. This cold embrace steals the last of my air as I start to grow exhausted. Dropping down to the depths below my last thoughts are of Atticus.

CHAPTER 7
MEDUSA

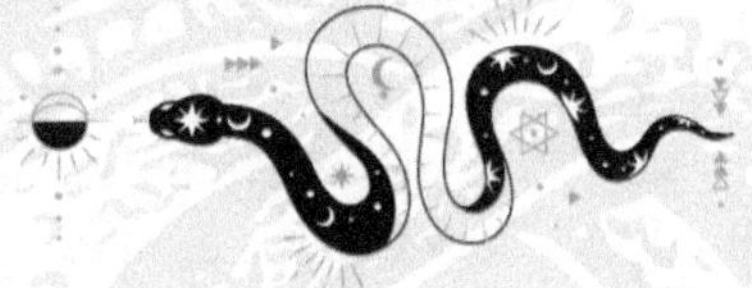

A spray of warm water hits my face, stirring me from my sleep, my body aches like it's been run over by a herd of Aequilla's. My head is fuzzy, hell even my eyelids ache. Taking in a few deep breaths I slowly open my eyes. I have no idea where I am, I feel disorientated and foggy. Where the hell did Zeus toss me? And how on earth am I meant to get back home?

I'm startled from my musings when I see several snakes staring at me, before I attempt to wrangle the creatures out of my hair. Instead, the crafty creatures curl tightly into my hair. After a few moments of taking in these stubborn slithering noodles trying desperately, but without much success to detangle them from where they have woven themselves in my hair, I decided to leave them be while I get my bearings and I crawl up the beach, flopping down on the black sand.

As I suck in a few steadying breaths, before taking my hand and try to untangle the snakes from my unruly mane of hair once more, except I am still unable to get them out. Oh well they'll slither their way out when I go to sleep, no creature snakes or otherwise want to be crushed by a goddess as she tosses and turns in her sleep.

Giving up, I take in the deserted beach, wondering where the hell I am. The only thing I'm sure about is that I am no longer in Karpathos. Looking to the right of the beach I look up and take in the large black stones making up the cliff face overlooking the sea. Large cavernous openings made into the rock, some opening out to a large deck built over the steep edge, a set of stairs, a mixture of metal and cliff built into the side of what looks to be someone's personal home leading down to the beach.

Looking up higher I see even more openings into the onyx stone, some that look open but if you look closely, you can see windows. A fact made known by the naked body pressed against the glass, someone behind him clearly enjoying his body. Feeling my face heat, I continue my perusal of the place; at the top of the cliff, I see a large lone house. Taking in my surroundings, the placement of the house, the cove I find myself in surrounded by lush green jungle, I appreciate the peaceful privacy someone has put a lot of thought into.

"How did I get here?" I wonder to myself, out loud.

"We'd like to know that, as well." I hear someone behind me say, his voice deep and smooth, like velvet.

Startling a little at the unexpected visitor, I turn to face the stranger. I try standing to face off against the new threat. Pain radiates up my leg causing me to cry out as I collapse back down onto the sand. Taking a deep breath in, I hold it for a few seconds before releasing it out. Repeating that several times massaging the sting in my leg till the cramping subsides. Movement out of the corner of my eye reminds me of the fact I am not alone and am now an easy target.

Standing before me is tall, dark, and deadly himself,

Hades, king of the underworld. His dark hair with wisps of smoke, a dead giveaway. Not to mention Karpathos has all kinds of promotional advertisements with him and his brothers on almost any surface. I'll admit when I was younger, I found it creepy seeing their faces in the bathroom stalls advertising their alcohol at the clubs Atticus had dragged me to. It was like the kings could watch you at all times from the pictures.

Gazing up at Hades I notice he isn't alone. Two other men flank each of his sides. To the right of Hades stands a tall, gorgeous man with long white hair, gray stormy eyes and a muscular build. The type of guy that could crush a stone wall with the flick of his fingers.

The male to the left of Hades has dark chocolate hair, while not as tall as the other, he is stockier, with large hands that look like they've seen a fighting ring or fifty. He is close to the same height as Hades but that's the only similarity. I can sense all three are powerful in their own right, each able to hold their own in a fight.

Locking eyes with them I feel something inside me wake, something primal that had never been there before. A need to walk over and mark them - a voice whispering mine, mine, mine, MINE. It's rhythmic tattoo, relentlessly beating its constant hammer of noise deep inside my aching skull, spearing its way through my body and deep within my soul.

Feeling the start of a pounding headache, I close my eyes to block out the light and avoid the dizziness that feels like it's taking over me. The ability to think clearly or with any sort of logic completely deserts me. I don't know if it's the heat or the seawater I swallowed from my impromptu dip, but I know my mind needs a break as the edges of my vision starts to blacken.

CHAPTER 8
EVERETT

The woman seems to melt before our eyes, Hades' jaw tenses as he looks over at me.

"Everett, pick up the girl and let's get home. Hopefully then we can get answers from our new guest." Hades orders before making his way up the cliff side, the stone path we built into the side for easy access to the beach that lies below our home.

The mansion, a modern masculine masterpiece built into the cliff, is an architect's wet dream. The inside, an open concept with a ton of natural light, modernized and eco-friendly. It was important to Octavius to make sure that everything was ecologically sound, adding plants for a modern meets' nature feel. The inside was several stories below, but you'd never know it from the outside. The front of the house is a large contemporary ranch with floor to ceiling windows, and black metal beams. The open concept necessary for our large, unusual family, but with a ton of privacy, our lot on the remote side of the island.

"Cooper, why don't you run ahead and grab Taura in

case she has any hidden injuries," I say before taking a tentative step towards our guest, while the snakes on her head watch my every move, hissing a warning.

"Please don't bite me, I'm only going to help her into the house." I tell them, they nod all at once creepily. Carefully leaning forward while keeping an eye on them, I slide an arm under her knees and wrap the other around her waist. Slowly I stand up trying not to jostle her too much. Lifting her with ease, noting how tiny of a thing she is.

I'll admit this woman was not what we expected to find laying on our beach. We felt someone breach our carefully placed wards, these magical barriers impenetrable unless given magical permission from its creator. Assessing the level of threat, Hades, Cooper, and I went to survey the area breached. Spying the temptress talking to her hair I couldn't help but walk forward to get a better look. Without realizing it, my legs led me closer, until she happened to look up and notice us standing there. Surprised that Hades allowed this beautiful being into our home and not the dungeon first for interrogation, shows me I am not the only one affected by her mere presence.

Pulling her close to my chest, my beast pushes closer to the surface, inhaling her scent and cataloging it for the future. I roll my eyes inwardly as he memorizes her scent for "research purposes". I see him mentally planning and mapping out the potential room Hades will put her in, and all the ways he can entice her out and into our room. My Gargoyle has already decided she's ours and is already planning the best nesting materials to entice her.

Internally, I roll my eyes at his antics, he's acting more like a phoenix with his possessiveness as we carry the enchantress to our home. Suddenly warm scales graze my face, I abruptly stop just as one of her snakes lick my cheek, while another slides up my neck.

"You promised no biting," I remind them while at the same moment the temptress in my arms buries her face against my chest.

"*Ours.*" my beast growls through our mind.

CHAPTER 9
ACE

Lounging in my favorite chair attempting to read, while waiting impatiently for the guys to come back from their investigation. They had told the rest of us not to worry and if they needed us, they'd let us know. I look at the clock, noting that they have three minutes left before I head down there to check on them. Shaking my head, I turn back my focus to the book in my hands when I hear a sudden 'bang' the door swinging open, slamming into the wall.

Hades enters first, grumbling as he makes his way into the room heading straight for the mini bar in the corner. I can hear Cooper in the hall yelling for Taura to get dressed and get her ass down here. Hades is pouring a glass of his favorite amber liquid, Death's Sins from our own private distillery in the underworld.

"Where is Everett?" I ask, walking over to Hades. The grumpy god doesn't answer me as he starts to down the drink. I roll my eyes standing there waiting for his dramatic ass to finish.

"Everett is fine, the girl, on the other hand, is, well, a mystery."

"Girl?" I ask, feeling a little intrigued.

"He means sexy snake goddess." Cooper fills me in from the door as he walks in to join us, grabbing the glass I had just filled, and downing it.

"What exactly did she do to you all that's making you drink whiskey like water?" I ask, feeling like I'm missing something huge.

"Get the rest of our bonded," Hades says as he makes his way over to the fireplace. I nod, rushing off to grab Kyrell, Octavius, and Garen. My mind reeling over what could have them acting so strangely. I pass Taura, giving her a smile, before making my way down to our bonding suite. Garen, Octavius and Kyrell had run down there earlier after their workout to shower before getting started on dinner. The closer I get to our suite the more I know exactly what these three are up to as Garens sweet cinnamon and cloves scent fills the air. His arousal is a special perfume instantly making me hard, luring me into our room.

I open the door and the sight of my bonded mixed with their combined arousal makes me greedy with lust. I take them all in, a sexy display of sin on our large bed. Octavius laying on his back with his hand guiding Garen's head up and down on his thick length, while Kyrell slides his wet dick into Garen's delectable ass.

Not ready to end this intimate moment to return back to what I am sure is going to be a long night of questioning our guest, I make the executive decision to join my mates before having to return upstairs to business. Quietly I shut the door before sprawling out on the large lounge on the other side of our room. Unbuttoning my pants and pulling the zipper down, my hard length springs free from its confines.

I begin to stroke myself in time with their pace, feeling the pleasure flowing through our bond.

"Garen, look what your pheromones are doing to Ace, I bet he is just thinking about how tight your ass feels," Kyrell says to Garen, making him moan louder as his eyes lock onto mine.

"Maybe if you are a good boy, and beg nicely, Ace will let you suck his cock." Kyrell adds and I smirk, slowing my pace as I wait for Garen.

"Garen, is that what you want? Do you want to suck my long, thick cock?" I tease, standing and walking over to the bed. Octavius moves off to the side, smiling and slowly fisting his own dick as he watches us.

"Don't get too comfortable, Octavius you are next," Kyrell says with a growl.

"I wouldn't have it any other way, love," Octavius replies with a wink.

I stand just off to the side, stroking myself slowly, Garen's eyes following the movement. Licking his lips, Garen begs "let me taste you Ace," releasing a frustrated moan Kyrell smirks, slamming a few more times into him while I circle the bead of cum from my tip around Garen's lips.

All three of my bonded watch me. I smirk, stepping out of my shoes, pulling down jeans and boxers slowly, before slipping my shirt off over my head. I step onto the bed, before kneeling before Garen. "Go on, taste him," Kyrell says as he slides his dick out of Garen's ass before crawling over to Octavius. Octavius grabs Kyrell's neck, pulling him down on top of him in a possessive kiss. Smiling, I turn my gaze back to see Garen's tongue slip past his pouty lips, as he seductively crawls towards me.

Once close enough, Garen wraps one hand around my

erection. Sliding it down around my base before lowering his head, flattening his tongue under the sensitive tip, a moan escaping my lips while the greedy man licks up the pre-cum.

"How do I taste?"

"Like you are mine," Garen replies, in a husky voice before his tongue glides over my shaft in firm strokes. Garen smirks before he takes me fully into his mouth.

"Fuck." I moan out as he picks up his pace, taking my length deep in his throat. Lacing my fingers in his hair, I start to thrust my hips, fucking his mouth harder and faster. Garen starts humming and sucking, it's fucking magical what he can do. It feels so good, but at the same time, it's not enough. I need more. Pulling his head back, I lean down, pressing my lips to his in a bruising kiss, biting his lip as I pull away.

"Turn around," I growl with need. Garen does as he is told, dipping forward so his ass is in the air. He wiggles it around a little, tempting me to give him a nice firm slap. I know I'm in for a treat tonight, with this sex-addicted vixen. My large hands cup his ass cheeks, giving them a hard squeeze.

"Behave, love." I say as I slide into him with a blunt promise, his ass still lubed and ready to go from Kyrell. Penetrating deeply, I bury my long-length, balls-deep in his tight ass. With my erection filling Garen, deep rumbling vibrations start to pulse through his body as I begin to move inside him.

"Harder." Garen moans.

"Anything for you, my mate," I growl as I slowly pull back out of him before thrusting myself home. I start moving again. Picking up my pace I piston into him, my cock ruthless. His body meeting my strokes eagerly, fueled by his own passion. Hunger matching hunger, our bodies come together, driving into my mate with an animal-like ferocity. Our groans fill the air, joining our other bonded, as we all chase our releases.

"Stroke your cock, Garen," I growl pulling him up, his back flush against my chest so I can watch his seed spill. I buck faster into Garen, his head falling back against my shoulder, thrashing as our climax draws us closer to the apex of desire. I thrust deeper, faster before I burst in a bone-deep growl with one last pump, pleasure flowing through us, my seed spilling into Garen. His body, milking mine of every last drop.

"Looks like you've made a mess," I growl, lifting his hand to my mouth, licking the cum off his hand before I gently kiss his lips.

CHAPTER 10
HADES

I can feel the heat and lust pulsing through the connection I share with my bonded. Attempting to wrestle down my growing excitement I firmly adjust my erection, it takes everything in me to not rush down the stairs and lock us all in a room to continue the orgy. Just as I'm about to cave and tell Cooper and Everett to join us in the room, the mirror on the wall starts to smoke up just before I see Hecate's face show up.

"Now what." I ask.

"What's got your panties in a bunch? Never mind, don't want to know. I just wanted you to know everything here is fine, but the Fates paid me a visit."

"Fuck, what did they have to say?" I ask, needing to know. The fates never pay a visit for fun. They always did it when someone was tipping the scales of power.

"Well, they were being very nice today and thankfully instead of their normal nonsense they told me we need to keep an eye on your brother Zeus, he is up to something big."

"Wonderful. Contact the few gods and goddesses we

can trust in Karpathos and see what kind of information you can get from them."

"Will do and Hades..." She pauses.

"Yes Hecate?" I ask my oldest friend.

"They also mentioned that if you find yourself with an unexpected guest, protect her." She says hastily before the mirror returns to its normal reflective status. I'm about to call her back and ask what she means by that. Before I get the chance Ace and the others are making their way into the office. All laughing and joking until they see my face.

"Hecate just called." I announce to the room.

"Is something wrong in the underworld?" Octavius asks.

"No, nothing like that. The fates just paid her a visit to warn me that Zeus is up to something again."

"Fucking hell. I swear if it's as bad as that time when he "borrowed" just "a few" cyclops' to hunt down Hera's secret lover I'm going to toss him into Tartarus with the rest of the fucktards."

"We are STILL cleaning up that mess." I say, thinking back on the incident when several cyclops went rogue and impregnated those donkeys. We are up to thirty-seven Donclops and while they're fairly harmless, they're annoying as hell- my thoughts trail off.

"There's only so many of those we can keep in the underworld without pissing off the other beasts." Garen reminds us all.

"If it comes to that, I will not stop you. I'll help you toss his ass in there and add a few Donclops for fun." Octavius snarks, ever so willing to get into a brawl. He's certifiably crazy the vast majority of the time, but that's one of the many reasons we all love him. He has the ability to see the fun and light in the darkest situations, making them easier to navigate. Internally rolling my eyes at his antics, I take a swig of my drink before moving onto more pressing matters.

"Now, hopefully Ace let you all know we have a guest on her way here with Everett. We don't know if she is a threat yet so keep your guard up just in case. At least until Kyrell can get a read on her."

"I second this. Now drink up before the snake goddess arrives." Ace says with a wink while Cooper snorts at Ace's use of his description of the woman.

"Well, here is to trusting the fates to know what they are doing." I mutter before downing my drink in a gulp.

CHAPTER II

ACE

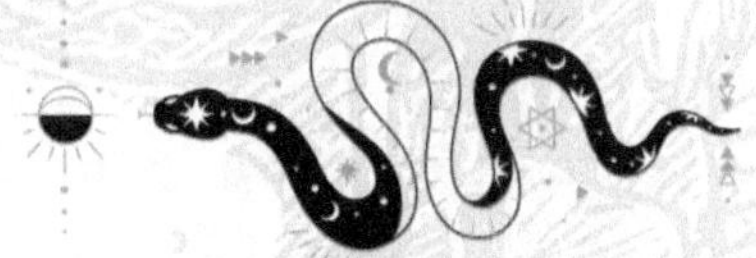

"How long does it take to get to the house?" Hades growls, pacing in front of the fireplace intermittently glancing towards the hallway, his hair now nothing but blue flames, a sign that he is feeling stressed.

"Calm down Hades, Everett is almost here with her," Kyrell says, all of us keeping an eye on Hades. He looks mere seconds away from exploding with frustration, and through our bond it feels even worse.

She must be something special to have the King of the Underworld this flustered. We all look up, upon hearing the front door open and close before one pair of footfalls echoes. I notice Hades has adopted a calm, carefree facade, conjuring up a fireball in his hand that he's tossing casually up in the air. Rolling my eyes, I stand with the rest of the guys on either side of the flustered god in a strong unified stance as we wait for them to enter the room.

Everett steps awkwardly into view cradling the tiniest woman in his arms. It takes a lot for me not to let loose the laugh I can feel bubbling up as I watch at least twenty snakes kiss and lick our bonded's face, while he is careful not to drop the petite goddess. Everett moves towards the couch with the girl. Once she is all settled, Everett moves aside waiting for Taura to assess her. She is the only female we allow to stay in our home.

Finding Cooper was like finding home, he just felt absolutely right. When Octavius had gone to the store for more rum, coffee, and cream. We hadn't anticipated he would come home with another mate plus a little sister. They had been living on their own for two years after the death of their mother. Even with Cooper working two jobs they were barely scraping by. Taking them in completed our family and gave us all the sister we never knew we were missing. She may be his blood, but she became our sister that day.

To my surprise, our new house guest feels right. A tendril of something unconsciously drawing me to her trying to reach out and latch on. Stopping myself as I feel my legs almost move subconsciously towards her, I mentally chastise myself, unsure if it's her power luring me into a sense of complacency or if it's something more. Feeling doubtful that the Fates could be that kind, to drop someone so perfect for us. I steel myself to what could be the coercion of her power.

CHAPTER 12
MEDUSA

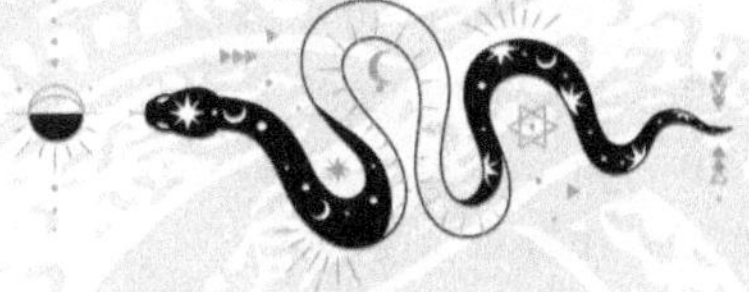

A buzzing of soft voices stirs me from the depths of my sleep. Something within urges me to wake up. Slowly opening my eyes, blinking a few times until they adjusted to the light in the room.

"Hi, my name is Taura."

"Medusa," I answer back as I try sitting up, Taura places a hand on my shoulder, stopping me from sitting up.

"You've been through a lot, you need to rest. I'm going to skim over you and try to heal what I can if that is alright?" Taura says.

Nodding, I take this moment in as I try to assess if she is dangerous or not. With beautiful creamy skin with enviable straight white hair, this beautiful being seems unfazed by my perusal of her. Dressed in an all-black ensemble with cute black bunny slippers, stylish and comfortable I immediately relax.

Evil doesn't wear bunny slippers.

Trying to feel for a creature under the surface of this being and coming up blank, I try coming up with what else she could be. Maybe a sorceress? Closing my eyes, I try once again to dive a little deeper to get a sense of power.

"Umm Medusa, can you open your eyes? I'm not quite sure what you're doing but my hands are hovering over your head and your snakes' eyes are doing some weird glowing purple thing that I'm not sure I can get down with at this time." snapping my eyes open, I feel my face burn as I stroke down my slithering coiling friends in an effort to smooth and soothe them.

"So sorry." I awkwardly laugh off, "Please continue".

"You seem to be healing, not relying so much on my powers, what were you thinking about?"

"Well, I don't want to be rude, but I was trying to get a feel for what you are, and I didn't know the exact etiquette of how to ask because we don't know each other," I say looking down at the floor timidly my snakes sheltering my embarrassed face. Laughing while reaching out to move one of the strands of hair out of my eyes, she says. "I am a sorceress, my brother and I come from a long line of magic users."

"That explains why I couldn't sense a creature." I give a little shrug. "But I appreciate your help."

"I'm going to ask you an odd question, and I don't want you to take offense but, something feels off about you." Taura starts, making me wonder what is coming next, a part of me is intrigued while the other part is fearful of her words.

"Your energy feels- not really like anything I've ever felt before. It's almost like your soul has been ripped apart and remeshed. One part of your aura, the part I'm assuming makes you a goddess is green. And the other is a color I would mostly associate with some of the beings from our island, more beast in nature. Both essences are melding together, as if they have not always been together, and I am just trying to figure out how the hell that happened. It feels new- Medusa have you not always been this way?"

"Wait, I don't understand what you mean?" I say more to myself than the audience around us. Trying to piece together the events leading up to waking up on the beach.

"It feels like you were cursed, but it feels different than any curses I've come across in my studies," Taura explains. " It would seem you are a shifter now. On the plus side you don't have to invest in expensive hair care products and your snake hair makes you look super exotic." she adds with a conciliatory smile.

"Snake hair? Surely you are jesting," I question. "They are just all tangled up in my hair, aren't they?" I question with sincere concern as I reach my hands up to check. Widening my eyes in surprise, I feel the smooth silky scales that coat the bodies of the nope ropes that are now attached to my crown in place of my familiar loose, green curls. One of the snakes I recognize from earlier curls around my hand and looks directly into my eyes with love and adoration so pure that I cannot be afraid of this alarming change.

My eyes lift up to find Everett standing over us hovering, before I look back at Taura. Questions fill my mind, my emotions feeling all over the place, anger and sadness crushing me. Taking a deep breath, closing my eyes for a moment. I need to calm myself before I explode. It feels like my life is crashing down all around me. How will this affect my powers? I begin to wonder if I will ever see Atticus and Suma again. Who will take care of my animals? What will happen to Loki? Will I ever be able to find my way home? While these guys may feel like home, I know that they aren't, and I am definitely not. Evercrest forest has always been home, and I will find my way back there.

Hissing from my hair brings me out of the shit storm that is raging in my mind. It's almost as though my snakes are responding to my inner turmoil and angst. I send them calming waves of love and reassurance, they're my snakes now! And like all the creatures I claim as mine I will protect them. As I open my eyes, I feel a smile crest my lips when I see two topaz eyes pop out from within Taura's hair, a cute little pink nose sniffing the air, its tiny feet bringing the creature into view.

I gasp in surprise as I come face to face with a wolpertinger, a rare creature that looks like a bunny with horns and small, opalescent wings. Taura notices what I'm looking at and grabs the little fluff ball off her shoulder.

"This is Pancake, my wolpertinger," she says holding him in her hands petting said ball of fluff.

"I know, I just haven't seen one since I was a kid," I say softly as I stick out my hand to let him sniff. When Pancake is close to me, one of my snakes moves closer, scaring the poor little guy causing him to take flight high above Taura.

"Sorry. "I reply to Taura. "They are just curious, they won't harm Pancake," I say, knowing deep down that statement is true.

"It's okay, he gets scared easily." She says while glancing up at the creature before turning her gaze back onto me, "but even with your wounds healing, you still need some more rest. Why don't I show you to the guest room so you can take a nap before dinner is done. It's Cooper's night to cook." She tells me as she looks over her shoulder smiling at the giant man from the beach.

A surprise gasp escapes my lips, while my feelings run wild in me as I take in the seven large male forms standing behind Taura leaning either against a large fireplace or leaning against furniture or the wall. I hadn't noticed them before, I'd been too distracted by my freak out. I turn away from their intense stares back to Taura's sweet smile.

"That would be lovely," I say while trying again to sit up. Slowly, I rise, my body groaning at the movement.

"Wait, we still have questions for her. How do we know she wasn't sent here to kill us?" Hades growls out.

"Seriously Hades!" Taura admonishes, "You would know very well if she was. Now I am going to show her up to her room where she can freshen up. You all can draw straws and decide which one of you big powerful men can stand guard outside her door if you are so concerned." she adds before facing me, "Come on Medusa I'll show you to the guest suite."

I stand, heading out of the door she is holding for me and start walking, stopping when I notice she isn't following me. Turning around I stifle a laugh as I take in the scene of her giving the guys the "I'm watching you" finger gesture. Before walking up to me and linking our arms like old friends, as we start heading up the stairs. Loud footsteps sound behind us causing me to jump. I turn to find Everett standing there.

"Mind if I tag along?" He asks us calmly, like he didn't just scare the life out of me. It takes me a moment to calm down. I like Everett, his presence is calming and solid. My instincts tell me, he is a safe haven that I can trust with my very soul. It tempts me and teases me, calling me to trust it and him. I want to take that chance and explore that sensation further.

"Not at all." I say at the same time Taura says "If you must."

Grinning Taura starts walking down the stairs, I'm a

little distracted, misstepping. Quickly I catch myself before
my face meets the beautiful black stone these are carved
from.

CHAPTER 13
MEDUSA

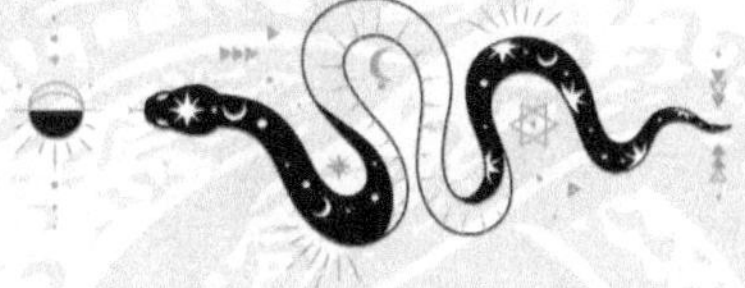

Taura doesn't waste time as she opens the first door on the right, I follow her into a large front room space with Everett right on my heels. I can practically feel his hot breath on my neck and his delectable scent of sandalwood and citrus. It's almost like my own personal calling card. I could breathe in all day, shaking my head clear while stepping away from the burly man, I am finally able to take in the room.

It's extravagant, with natural black stone walls of the cliff this place is carved from. The open concept living space has its own living room and cozy kitchen. Floor to ceiling windows brighten the space up while giving spectacular views of the beach and jungle. An emerald lounge chair placed perfectly in front, dares me to come rest on it, I can picture myself falling asleep staring out into the endless greenery. In the center of the room sits a gray couch shaped in a L so that whoever sits on it can get warmed up by the large fireplace that is on the wall to my right and still able to appreciate the view that this room is centered around. To the right of the living space an open door catches my attention.

"That door leads to the master bedroom with an adjoined bathroom. It should have everything you need for bathing."

"Thank you," I say, turning to find Everett so close by, that I nearly trip as I turn to check out the rest of the guest suite. Reaching out to steady me, Everett's arms stray up to my shoulders.

"My beast is enthralled with you. He is very curious and keeps pushing me to be closer to you so he can unravel your secrets." He whispers into my ear.

"Is he always so curious?" I question back as I try standing taller to face off with the giant man before me.

"Curious? Is that what the kids are calling it these days?" I hear Taura mutter with a chuckle. We both turn to look at her, but Taura isn't even fazed by Everett's glare; she just shrugs while smiling, her eyes ping ponging back and forth like we are the best entertainment she has seen in ages. I bet if she could, she would have popcorn while she watches the whole interaction.

Two fingers gently turn my face back but instead of staring into the storm gray eyes these one are completely silver, and I know that Everett has checked out while I am left to meet his gargoyle.

"Taura is family, but you feel like something more" he says with a slight growl to his voice that vibrates through my body making a warmth spread through me. Everett then steps back, his eyes closing as he seems to be waging an internal battle. When his eyes open again, I am staring back into familiar gray eyes, "Why don't you take a quick shower and by the time you get done there will be some clothes out by the door. I am not trying to intrude but my beast is struggling at the surface worried you might still be hurt. If you wouldn't mind, I'd like to stay to ensure everything is fine before I take my leave?"

I nod my head not sure what to say before I make my way into the bedroom, there are two other doors closed in here. I go to the first one to find it is a closet. Closing it, I head to the other one. I take a deep breath before I open it up. I'm frozen on the spot as I get my first glimpse of my new form. My breath hitches as I see my reflection, I hardly recognize the creature staring back at me. She is beautiful, wild, and free. The tendrils of snakes are small but many, their movements smooth and delicate causing it to look like my hair was constantly moving in a soft gentle breeze. My purple eyes now sparkle with a new magic. My skin is a little more golden and my lashes are longer.

Lifting a hand to my face, I wince when it makes contact with my cheek. A look of shock crosses my face as it hits me. This is really me. Exotic was the word Taura used to describe me, and she couldn't have said a more perfect word to describe the creature goddess hybrid I have become. When I'm able to look away I remember why I am in the bathroom to start with. Turning on the water, I breathe deep, closing my eyes as I take in everything that has happened to me. Tears stream down my face as I let my mind wander to the events that led me here.

My snake hair is rubbing against my face, giving me comfort. I soak it in as I give myself one more moment to fall apart. I let all of my anguish go, angry tears pouring from my soul. I wanted to scream, fight and punch at the injustice of it all.

Destiny is a bitch sometimes.

I cried till my tears ran dry, before undressing out of the remnants of my dress and sliding into the steaming hot shower. The heat does wonders for my sore muscles, giving me a moment of normalcy as I lather my body in the sweet vanilla and lavender soap. Rinsing away the last bits of sand and the remnants of salt from the ocean. Once I'm satisfied that I have scrubbed every inch of my body, I stand there enjoying the water for a few more moments. Reluctantly turning off the shower I step out, grabbing a fluffy gray towel from the wood shelves built into the wall next to the stone shower.

Drying off before I step back out to my bedroom, I breathe a sigh of relief when I see that Taura, or Everett, remembered to close the door to my room. A small smile tugs at the corner of my mouth as I spy a shirt and a pair of lounge pants laying on the bed. Picking up the shirt I bring it up to my nose breathing in the unique scent of sandalwood and citrus. Instantly I know which of the guys these clothes belong to. After getting dressed a few more tears break free just as I'm heading out of the room in search of some tea I can make before I get some rest.

Wiping my tear-stained cheeks, I pause in the doorway as a growl reverberates in the room. My eyes land on Everett, who is sitting on the lounge chair. His skin has taken on an ashen gleam, his silver eyes taking in my face, and he lets out another growl, his gargoyle overriding his normal self. Instantly, Everett is in front of me encasing me in his arms as something in me snaps. My silent tears turning from a gentle stream into a thunderous storm.

Everett carries me back into my room while I lose myself to my emotional breakdown. He tucks me into the soft blankets pulling me back into his embrace. Letting me ruin his shirt with my tears.

"**D**id that really just happen?" I ask, still staring after my sister as she disappears from sight with Medusa and Everett trailing after them.

"*I'll take first watch.*" Everett says through our bond I swear I can hear his smug smile through the link.

We all just sit there lost in our thoughts till Hades clears his throat as one we all look over at him. "We need to tread lightly around our guest. I know you all can feel her lure, she might not outright want to hurt us but till we know more about her I say we keep her a friendly arm's length away."

This whole thing is a test of wills from the ancients, I doubt any of us will survive unfazed from this mess. I stand making my way over to the bar in the corner grabbing one of the crystal glasses I fill it full of Death's Sins. Downing the drink in one go. Before the burning liquid can even finish its trek down my throat, I am pouring another.

"We must have really pissed off the ancients for them to test us like this." I grunt out as I look over my shoulder at my bonded. As if they could hear all my thoughts, their faces mirror everything that is running through my mind. We've all been through so much over the years and something tells me this test will be the worst one yet. I turn back to my drink bringing the glass back up to my lips. I tilt my head back savoring the burn as it helps to calm my inner magic. Magic that is reaching out for the one who may end up being our sweetest prize. I feel thick arms band around my waist, as I'm pulled back against a solid chest.

"I trust your judgment to be able to get the truth out of her, for now we just need to stay alert." Hades whispers in my ear nipping my neck making me groan. "So responsive," he purrs as he continues his assault on my neck, his hand trailing down my chest towards my cock that has been rock hard since my eyes landed on the snake goddess we found on the beach.

If not for the fact that it would be a disgrace to my bonded and our center when we find her, I would have taken her right there on the beach. The moment Hades hand touches over my restrained cock I thrust up into his hand, then without another thought I make all of our clothes vanish.

"Please give a girl a warning before you make her brother's clothes disappear." I hear Taura complain before I hear her feet retreat down the hall towards the kitchen.

"Let's all take this to our shared room, I feel like some of us need to blow off some steam," I say chuckling at Taura's retreat, not caring enough at the moment to worry about what my sister may have seen. Releasing some of my magic I instantly bring our all to our room. The moment we appear I'm pushed up against the wall upon entering our chambers.

"Tell me what you need Cooper," Hades demands.

"Make me forget her." I beg, knowing that it will be impossible to completely forget the snake goddess we've brought into our home. Her spiced vanilla and jasmine scent lingers, wafting from the office we were just in.

"As you wish." Hades replies as he takes my cock in his fist and starts stroking it. I hear the others moving and some grunting. I peek my eyes open to see Ace sucking off Garen while Kyrell is bent over a chair. I watch as Octavius pushes his cock into his ass and starts thrusting in and out hard and fast.

Hades releases his hold on my aching cock pushing me forward. With my precum coating his fingers, I feel him inserting one of his digits into my ass slowly as he moves it in and out before adding another teasing me. This slow build up is complete torture. Tapping into our bond he feels my impatience, he pumps them in and out pulling them out completely and filling me with his large cock, the piercings on the underside of his dick leading to an ampallang on the tip add to my already over sensitive canal.

"Don't hold back," I growl out as I start moving.

"I won't." he replies, and I can almost hear the smile in his voice before he sets a fast and hard pace. Unable to stand the lack of pressure on my cock I start stroking myself at the same brutal pace that Hades has set. Hades seems to notice I am holding back, he whispers in my ear.

"Did you think I wouldn't pick up on your lust for our new houseguest? Can you imagine her reaction to me pushing you against the window and putting you on display for her? She caught sight of Garen and Kyrell fucking against the window when she woke up on the beach. Her face heated in embarrassment, but the smell of her arousal hasn't left me." With that image, I burst, growling out an orgasm like none I've had before, taking Hades over the edge with me as my ass milks his dick for everything it's worth.

ATTICUS

"Atticus it will be alright man." Luri says as he sits next to me on the ground.

I glare at him from the corner of my eye, "you couldn't possibly understand."

"Try me." He says grabbing an apple and holding it out for Loki or Jezebel to take. Neither one looks happy. They have barely eaten any of the food I've prepared for them, so much misery emanates from them, it's almost so palpable it has physical form. It mirrors my own heart ache. We've all been struggling since losing her.

"She is my mate."

"Hold up! Rewind. Medusa was your mate?"

"Still is." I correct, "She isn't dead, I can still feel it in my soul. She is only lost to me." With a shake of his head, he rushes inside the house. I can hear him rustling in the kitchen. Whack' something round hits me in the back of my head. I turn to see my friend with an arm full of oranges and apples.

"Get the fuck out of here and go find your mate." Luri curses at me, like he thinks I am so stupid for not leaving to find her before now. Who knows maybe I am. I have been a lost wreck since she was taken, listlessly moving through the motions as I try to fight my way through the depression that has been gripping its claws as deeply as possible into me since she's been gone.

"I can't leave Loki and the other animals." Which is true if I ever found her again Medusa would kill me if anything happened to Loki, Jezebel, and Lulu. Though even knowing the truth of what I have just said, it feels like a weak excuse even to my own ears. Of course, right then my mother appears from nowhere to stand next to Luri.

"We've got the animals covered." She tells me holding out her hand, in her grasp is a map. I take it from her, keeping a wary eye on my fruit throwing friend. Luri looks like he wants to pelt me out of my stupor and into action. The look he's giving me lights a fire under my ass, he's right, my mate needs me. Am I the God of the Sun and Moons or am I a floof masquerading as one?

"Thank you." I say to my mother before rushing into the cabin adding a few things in a bag and some weapons before I rush back out. I pull my mother into my arms. Somehow my mystical mother always knows what I need. I should have known better than to doubt it now.

"Find her Atticus she will need you, and the others' strength and guidance to get through the battles that lie ahead." my mother says patting my back calmingly. Giving me a final squeeze, she releases me. Her eyes, imploring me to find my mate and keep her safe.

"I will find her." I vow. I must! I need her, like I need the air I breathe. Failure is not an option. If I had been cursed and tossed off a cliff by an evil dick like Zeus, Medusa would give anything and everything in her quest to find me. How could I do any less for her? I can't! She stood by lovingly supporting me when Circe was controlling me with dark magic, unable to see the truth of what was going on, but wanting me to have the life she thought I wanted. Selfless, loving woman that she was.

"I love you, Atticus."

"I love you, Mother." I reply, hugging her tightly to me before letting her go.

When I pull away Luri is there with his arms open. "Don't leave me hanging." The corner of my mouth lifts as I reach out, pulling Luri into my embrace, squeezing too tight. "Call me if you need help, I'll keep your mother safe here." Luri says before I release him.

I nod, slipping the bag over my shoulder, releasing my wings before taking to the sky. The next time I come back here, it will be with Medusa by my side. No one will ever take her away from me ever again.

CHAPTER 16

MEDUSA

It's hot. Way too hot, I need cold air, a snowstorm, something to cool me down. When I try sitting up I can't, something huge is holding me down. Panic settles in as I start to claw at my blanket.

"Calm yourself little goddess." Everett whispers in my ear before I feel him nuzzling into my neck. Instantly his scent of sandalwood and citrus bombards my system causing me to relax. At least until the days leading up to this perfect moment flash through my mind again.

Everett turns me on the bed without releasing his hold on me. Both of us are laying on our sides with our bodies angled towards each other. This feels so intimate, yet it terrifies me how my body molds perfectly into his hold. A buzzing intensity filters between us. My body heat increases, as fluttering butterflies go crazy in my belly. I bite my lips, hoping he can't sense how bad I want to kiss him to see if his lips are as soft as they look. The attraction I am feeling towards him is strange yet being wrapped in his arms makes me feel like I've always belonged here with him and the others.

Like I've finally come home.

Our heads turn as my suite door is slammed open. "Where are you, my lovely goddess?" I hear a slightly accented voice call out. Everett's hold on me tightens, just as another one of the guys from downstairs strolls into the bedroom.

"Don't you two look comfy. Is this brooding statue bothering you, love? I could have him leave so we could get to know one another better." He says jumping swiftly onto the bed at my feet, laying on his side. Everett growls low in his chest before pulling me closer to him as he glares at his friend like he is a pest he just can't seem to get rid of.

"Octavius behave," Everett growls out.

I pat Everett's chest and smile softly at him. "No, he's been extremely sweet." I answer, still unsure what to make of these men. My instant attraction to all of them is the biggest question. Back in Karpathos I only had eyes for Atticus. Sure, I had tried dating a few other gods which mostly led to disappointment, especially on the occasions I had slept with them. The men only seek out their own pleasure, leaving me hanging. After that I decided I didn't want anyone who didn't want me for more than a rumble in the sheets. Aside from all that I still find it strange how nice they are all being to me. Was this normal for them? Or was it perhaps a game they all played with unsuspecting females who happened to cross their paths? I couldn't help but be a little cautious in case it was some kind of trap Zeus set up.

"Well, I think it is time we get up and go see if dinner is ready," Everett says with a sweet smile.

"Or I could stay and cuddle with her. Would you like me to stay and keep you company, love?" Octavius says with a wink. My imagination has no trouble filling my mind with images of me squished in-between both these men as we cuddle in bed. Before I even get a chance to politely decline his tempting offer my stomach gives out a hangry snarl.

"I do believe your stomach has given us its input." Everett says, as he releases his hold on me.

"Well, I'm sure if I do not get some food soon it will take over and have me trying to eat all of you." I joke as I get off the bed.

"I have no quarrels over that plan. What about you Octavius?" Everett groans out as his eyes have taken on the silver hue, I am starting to recognize as his gargoyle.

"None at all love." Octavius replies.

Unsure what to do or say, my mouth suddenly shouts, "BATHROOM." just before running into the bathroom and shutting the door. When I flick on the light, I find that I ran into an empty closet.

I wrench open the door and scurry to the bathroom and close it quickly as laughter from the two men still out in my bedroom rings through the air. Sexy jerks! How dare they laugh at my embarrassed discomfort. Taking a breath, I mentally ask my snake hair if they have any powers we can use to make them forget what just happened. To my disappointment we don't.

Sighing with relief before I stand and flush the toilet, turning on the tap I grab the white soap with pieces of lavender melted into it. Rubbing the buttery soft soap between my hands till they are covered in bubbles. I set it back down on its dish before rinsing away the soap. Cupping my hands, I then splash a little water on my face to help freshen it up.

Opening the top drawer I smile, while pressing my hands together, "thank you fates," I whisper when I see a toothbrush and minty toothpaste sitting there.

Quickly I attack my bad morning breath, once I am

satisfied with that task and have rinsed and placed my meager belongings back in the draw. Yes, that toothbrush is mine now. I take a deep breath trying to ground my chaotic self before turning to face the door.

I know I need to go out there, but I feel a little overwhelmed. All of these changes in my life are taking place. I don't know where I belong or what to do with my life now. Taking a moment to clear my mind, I need to get everything sorted, stay maybe another night, before I find a job and new housing arrangements. I don't know if I'll ever be able to return home now, especially in my current state, with what Zeus did to me. I need to come up with a plan, I need to figure out this new form and all of the powers that accompany it. Once my thoughts are somewhat clear I make myself leave the safety of the bathroom.

"Ready to go eat?" Everett asks me.

"Yes," I say just as my stomach grumbles its agreement.

CHAPTER 17
HADES

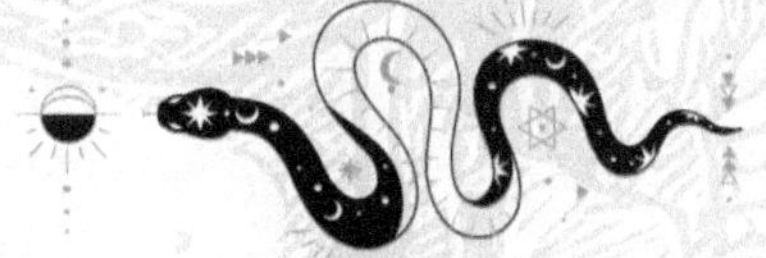

Still feeling conflicted about our guest, is she the one Hecate told me to protect or is she another trick from my brother? I'll admit she is a tempting morsel. As if summoning the temptress with that thought alone, she enters the room. Her arm linked with Everetts as they stroll into the dining room. Her gaze ensnares me immediately as a delicate smile appears. Everett pulls out her seat, one that is next to me on my right and across from Kyrell. Something we had talked about earlier as we got dinner made.

"So, Medusa if you wouldn't mind, I have a few questions for you that I figured would be best to ask over dinner."

"Ask away," she says as a bowl of soup is set down in front of her along with two fresh baked rolls on a small plate. Instantly I'm distracted as I watch as she dips her spoon into the bowl and then brings it up to her lips while I dish up my own food. When she takes her first bite of food, the moan that left her mouth has me choking on air in surprise. A few grumbles and grunts echoed around the table let me know I wasn't the only one affected by her.

She lifts her head to look over at me," Are you okay?" She asks in a whisper. I nod, waving her off and take a bite of my food.

"Damn, that was sexy," Garen says in our bond, making me choke again only this time on my food. It's a miracle that it doesn't come back out of my nose.

"It definitely was, do you think if I bring food to her in bed, I'll be able to hear some more of those moans?" Octavius says as he stares at her like she's the last piece of food on a deserted island.

"You guys, okay?" Medusa asks.

"Yes," I say with a cough which gets the others to look back at their plates or start conversations with each other.

"Medusa," I say, catching her attention again.

"Yes Hades?" she says looking over at me with her bright amethyst eyes. With her eyes looking at me like that my mind goes blank. To buy myself time I grab my glass and take a sip of my whiskey, *"be nice,"* Everett chastises through our bond.

"I will be but don't forget we all should be weary, this wouldn't be the first time a beautiful woman has been dropped onto our land. My brother likes to send one or more to entrap us into a false bond with a center. Something that would weaken us enough for the psycho to swarm in and invade the island."

Cooper sighs, *"We remember, it's something we've kept Taura in the dark about."*

"No need to worry her about something that hasn't been an issue." Garen adds in.

"That is till today." I start, **"While I am not blind, I can see that Medusa has an alluring effect on us all. And as of right now we don't know if she is another trick."**

"Hades, is everything okay?" Medusa asks as she lays

her hand on top of mine. No one says anything, they don't even dare to breathe as they watch what my reaction will be.

I nod my head, "Yes everything is great." I answer Medusa even gracing her with a sweet smile.

"Wanker." Octavius says under his breath, causing Ace to start choking on his drink. Fuck this is a mess. In my head this all went so much simpler, we'd eat, and I'd ask her questions. Kyrell would let me know if she told the truth or not and then we'd decide if she is another trick or maybe destiny's long-awaited gift.

"Why don't you tell us how you landed on our beach love?" Octavius asks as he pours her a glass of fae wine. Medusa takes a sip of her drink while we all wait for her answer.

"I'm not sure what exactly happened. I was enjoying the ball with my friend Atticus. Then suddenly it felt like I was being burned from the inside out. So much pain, the next time I came to, Zeus was preparing to toss me off a cliff and then I woke up here." Medusa's gaze is far away from us like she is trying to turn back time.

Without even having to look over at Kyrell, "*truth.*" He answers. We all hold our breath waiting for her to say more. When Medusa doesn't, I ask my next question even if my heart is screaming for me to stop. But I can't risk my bonded to save the feelings of someone who might lead us to our end.

"Are you in any way using an allure on us?" I ask her.

Medusa turns to me with surprise written across her face, "I would never intentionally use any sort of allure on anyone. But with the new changes in me I have no clue if I am or not. If so I am so sorry and once I can figure out my new gifts I'll make it stop." She replies, now looking down at her hand, biting her lip as she seems to be searching within herself to find an off button.

"Truth." Kyrell says. My body instantly releases the large ball of stress that I didn't realize I was holding onto.

"Also as soon as I can I'll move out into my own place." Medusa announces. My head snaps up to look back at her as I feel unhappy about her leaving. This isn't normal. We should be glad she has no problem leaving to begin her new life. But through the bond I can feel how the others don't want her to leave us. My suspicion is raging through the roof now. I'll have Ace keep an eye on our new guest from the shadows.

"I understand how overwhelmed you must be feeling, you can stay here until you get on your feet," I say magnanimously, my intentions not completely pure, wanting to keep her close so we can continue observing her. Just because it's not an allure she is using on us, doesn't mean it isn't something else.

CHAPTER 18
MEDUSA

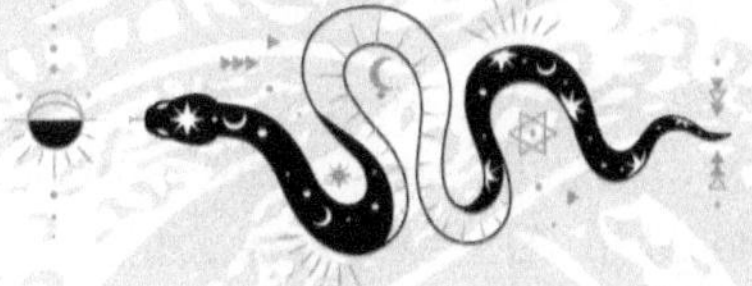

Taura and I walk out of the room, chatting softly with each other, leaving the guys to clean up dinner.

"So, are you dating any of the guys?" I inquire, instantly wishing I could take back the words and ask about anything else.

Taura burst out laughing. "No, that would be so wrong. Besides, no one wants to see their brother getting his rocks off with all his bonded."

"Bonded?" I ask as my curiosity gets the better of me. What does the term mean? I can take a guess, but if it means anything like I think it does, what does that mean for how they have been flirting with me?

"Bonded is a name for a group of males." Just a group of males I desperately wanted to ask. What sort of group? Why did it feel like Taura was being deliberately obtuse? I mean I knew she wasn't, but for some reason I couldn't quite explain, something told me this conversation was important.

"Do they not each have their own mate?" I ask as we

reach the door to my room. Taura opens the door passing through the living room and walks straight into the kitchen standing in front of the sink, with a flick of her wrist the kettle off the stove floats right over to her waiting hand, she then fills it up before sending it back to the stove that turns on.

"Well, for us, monsters usually mate in groupings. Each group is individualized, each partner bringing something different to the table. Almost like puzzle pieces. For us, back in the day women were few and far between, so packs formed together to ensure protection. Long ago many lost themselves to their beast. Beasts running rampant in their desperation to fight for and find a mate to balance them, were very destructive and lethal to others. Lessening the female population, which was already small, even more.

Males of different species came together out of survival, each having different powers and ways to safeguard their mate. The female in turn acts as what we call a center, a way to stabilize our beasts not just giving a huge power boost but also grounding our beasts so that we don't become feral.

While life has evolved, and feral monsters have decreased the center bond is revered. The special connection and bond give powers and abilities unique to their own group. It is even more rare and revered to have a fully centered group in this age, because there hasn't been one in a very long time. Some say that evolution worked its way out and made centers obsolete."

Taura turns to grab the kettle off the stove as it starts screaming at the same time two teacups come floating out of the cupboard along with tea bags, they settle themselves on the counter next to Taura. She pours the water and sets the pot back down on the stove.

"Would you like cream and sugar?" She asks, looking over her shoulder at me.

"Yes please." I reply as I watch the fridge open, and the cream comes floating out while she drops two scoops of sugar into my cup and hers. The cream pours itself before floating back into the fridge. Taura walks over towards the couch, I turn and follow her.

"So sometime soon we're going to have to take you shopping, but for now I have some clothes you can borrow. I know you've been through a lot of new changes lately, so why don't we just take the next few days to relax and get your bearings?" Taura says.

"That sounds like a really good idea to me, I can't thank all of you enough for taking me in, thank the fates I landed on your guys' beach" I say sincerely.

"It feels like the Fates had a hand in where you ended up. I'm glad you landed here too. We could use a little excitement around here, and I feel like you're just the right person. Now I don't know about you but I'm pretty tired. Let's head to bed so we can start the day early."

CHAPTER 19
ATTICUS

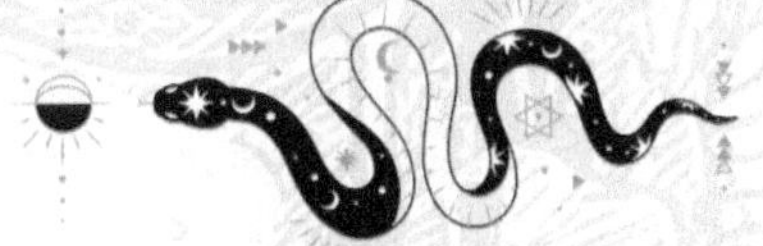

Who knew mermaids could be so sneaky with traps. Hell, I didn't even know they could walk on land at any time they pleased. I was wrong, so wrong, and now my life is in the hands of a little mermaid no older than seven.

"I can't believe it. I caught a god. You know, Wava said that I'd never catch anything with my nets. She is going to be so jealous that my nets worked and hers didn't." She tells me with her sweet twinkling voice. "I need to go get my father so if you could just stay here, I'd love to show him how well my trap worked." She explains before running off into the trees before I can even reply.

Honestly, like, where am I going to go? At least I can check off Oceania Isle after this visit. Thankfully, while waiting for the little mermaid to return I am able to retract my wings back into me, giving myself a little more room in my net. But not much. I feel like a fool for falling for such a childish trick. But my mind recently has not been my own.

Time ticks by slowly and my thoughts wander back to Medusa. As much as I hope she is here, I try not to get my hopes up. Though if my sweet mate had washed up on any shore this one would be one of the more pleasant ones. The mermaids aren't a threat to others unless they are forced. I do remember my mother telling me when I was a child how she had once met mermaids in her youth.

She explained they were cautious supernaturals but not violent. Unlike their siren sisters, they are normally the warriors of the merpeople. All merpeople can be quite deadly. Swimming fast and soundless, with voices that lure you into a trance before they rip your throat out. At least that's how the gods explained them. But now after my travels I'm starting to see some inconsistencies in the stories. A lot actually, almost like they were created to keep most of the young gods like myself from exploring other islands. Occasionally at the balls some fae royals would attend and ages ago the dragon shifters. But now it was an island consisting of gods and goddesses. Most of who are tyrants on our realm including our selfish leader. I'll never understand how or why Zeus ever became the ruler he is without being taken down by some of the other more powerful beings.

I let my thoughts drift from less important topics back my top priority, my search for Medusa. Overall, the islands that Medusa could have landed on, and what one I'd need to search next if she isn't here. I am a little embarrassed to say that, while raising the sun and moon with my mother, I never put much thought into keeping track of the islands we rode over in our flying chariots. Instead, I focused more on getting my job done so we could return home.

At some point, I must have drifted off to sleep. When I awoke, I noticed hours had passed since my little captor scampered off. A rainbow of oranges, blues and yellows fill the sky in the distance as the sun sets at the end of another day. Some rescuer I am. At this point, Medusa would have a better chance at finding me than I would her. The sounds of whispers reach me. I try sitting up to see who is approaching, but whoever it is, is lying out of my sight.

"He can't hurt us, Mother." I hear the familiar twinkling voice of my captor say.

"He is a god, Muriel, we need to tread carefully." Another deep voice replies back in a warning.

"He didn't harm me, Father," she replies, making me chuckle. She is right, I could have ended her life if I had wanted to. But I'm not that kind of God. I decide this is my only chance to show them I am no threat.

"I give you my word I won't harm your blood, or your friends Muriel." I announce so my words can be heard by anyone with her, as my intention is true, I can feel the ancient magic told hold of my promise sealing my promise. "I am just looking for my mate, she was cast out to sea, and I am worried for her safety."

Suddenly, a tall slim figure steps out of the trees, his long emerald hair flows down his back. He holds a gold trident in his hand. His artic-blue eyes take me in as if he is trying to decide if my words are the truth or lie so that they will set me free.

"And what does this mate of yours look like?" He asks.

"She was cursed, but before that, she had long green hair, amethyst eyes. Golden skin with high cheekbones, a dimple on her right cheek, with a dainty nose. Full lips with a cupid's bow, petite in height, curvy, yet slender. She is kind-hearted, has the power over nature to use at her will or grow plants, and communicate with animals." I tell him, my heart wrenches at the thought of never seeing her again. In an instant, the net I am in is falling to the ground.

"Muriel." the man growls.

"He can't hurt us, he promised." She tells him matter of factly.

"She is right, my love, besides, he isn't here to harm us or take anyone from us like the other gods do." A tall lithe woman says as she walks out from around a palm tree.

I stand rubbing my backside, the fall a little higher than I previously thought. I hold my breath while waiting for Muriel's father, who I assume to be their leader, to make a decision on my future. As if the fates heard my prayers, he gives me a nod.

"Fine, come with us, God. We will eat and help you figure out if your mate is among the many women and children who have arrived on our shores." He replies before turning and walking back into the trees. Muriel and her mother both smile before following after the king. Relief fills me with a small amount of hope that I am capable of finding Medusa.

CHAPTER 20
ACE

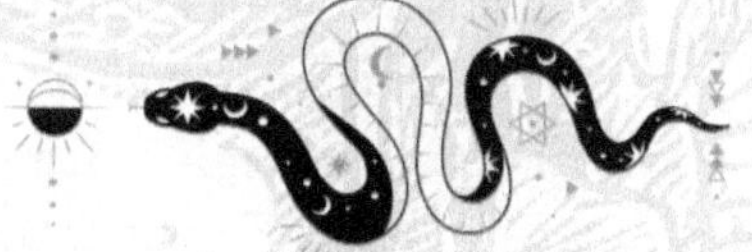

I couldn't help myself, drawn to her pain and fear tasting it on my tongue, immediately wanting more. As a shadow creature I was attracted to that darkness, eating it up like the sweetest dessert. My shadow abilities gifted me the ability to dream-walk, allowing me the option to feast on nightmares. I could liberate the dreamer from their personal hell, or exacerbate it, my dream walking abilities a blessing or curse depending on the recipient. A real live boogeyman, a nightwalker. I usually never spared the dreamer unless it was a mate, family, or friends, seeing as how I had no friends, I usually luxuriated in the fears of others, mostly preying on the evil.

The pain of her nightmare called to me like a siren. Drowning me with hunger that didn't seem quite right. That's how I found myself in her room, her tossing and turning concerning me, an emotion I've rarely ever felt, luring me to her side. The beast inside me, straining to get into her dream. Telling myself I'd take away her nightmare and then quickly leave, she'd never remember me there anyway. Dreamers never see me unless I will it so, and even then, they never remember me in their dreams.

Entering her dreamscape, I witness what must have been, what led her here. The pain and humiliation, the words Zeus spoke to her, just as she was thrown over the cliff. Her back to the sea, staring up at the sky as she fell. I yelled at her jumping in, and in that moment, I was lost. Her terrified eyes connect with mine. Catching her and pulling the dreamscape into a different setting, I conjured only the softest pillows and bedding. We land together in the dreamscape bed, just in time to avoid splashing into the icy water.

It takes me a moment to process what I have just done. But saving her felt so right, easing her pain and taking away all her fears, had sated my beast. He was settled and comforted in a way he never has been before. He doesn't thrive on her pain and fear like he would anyone else's, but rather her comfort and safety were important to him. It surprised me that my beast was so taken with her, so protective of her. It surprises me even more that I was too. I just wish I could have protected her from the scene I just witnessed when it had actually happened in the first place.

"Please don't leave me," she whimpers in a whisper.

"I would never." I say, I don't think I could even if I wanted to. Wrapping her tightly in the covers and pulling her back to my chest her small hand poked out of the sheet clasping my hand.

"Thank you for saving me," she says sleepily, holding my hand tightly like a lifeline and closing her eyes. Never before has anyone ever seen me and acknowledged my existence in their dreams. I hold her close as I process that, until I too fall asleep.

CHAPTER 21
MEDUSA

My mind is a hurricane of emotions, trying to piece together what exactly happened to get me to this point. A good portion of the night I spent tossing and turning before finally falling asleep. I must've wrapped myself tight enough in the covers to imitate a warm, cozy embrace. Comforting me allowing a false sense of security to fall over me and bring me into a deep slumber. Waking to a blast of sunlight shining through my windows, I know I'm never going to be able to fall back asleep. Turning to my right, I could've sworn I saw a shadow of something slide out of the door. Just as I head out of my room to investigate, I hear a few hard knocks.

Making my way to the door I open to find a smirking Taura, a disgruntled Everett, and a tall shirtless beast of a man covered in neck to torso, black ink markings made of the most intricate designs. My eyes begin feasting on the delicious V leading up to 6 pack abs, my eyes bugging as I take in the shiny barbells adorning his nipples.

Oooo shiny fancy nip nips come to mama.

Hearing the raucous laughter, my eyes bounce up to

meet his dancing with mirth, a smirk gracing his full lips. In that moment I've just registered I most definitely spoke that out loud, my face warm, and wearing my mortification for all to see. *"Damn all these sexy men, how dare they walk around so temptingly shirtless in their own home."* I snark in my head, hoping I don't also have drool running down my chin, just to add to the mortification of the situation.

"Alrighty *mama,* Everett and I were just stopping by to drop off a few things for you to wear to help get you through till we head to town. We're going to grab something to eat, and head down to the water for a relaxing beach day. We figured the goddess of creatures and nature would feel best outside getting some fresh air, *and* we just so happened to run into Ace right outside your door... *fancy that,"* Taura smiles slyly up at a scowling Ace. Moving out of the way, I let her and the guys in, grabbing one of the boxes she had floating behind her.

"I brought you the essentials, they all still have tags," whispering so the guys don't overhear she says guiltily, "I didn't have the heart to tell Octavius, our resident fashionista, that anything that is not black, dark black, midnight, or if I'm really desperate dark charcoal, isn't really my style."

Taura gestures the remaining five boxes full of "essentials" onto the table, and I turn to see the guys snickering as she heads over to the windows to look out. Turning a questioning brow at them Everett steps close to me whispering, "Octavius bought them as a joke, he's been trying to get her to wear something other than black ever since we met her and Cooper. We've got a bet going on and he's a pretty poor loser and won't accept defeat."

"And, I don't have the heart to tell him about the nightmares his monstrously bad fashion choices have been giving her." Ace gave a dark but sexy laugh, almost a chuckle. Everett joined in but Taura was not amused.

"Oh, so you know about my nightmares?" She was snarky as she shoots Ace a murderous glare.

"I walk in shadows and nightmares, I'm literally a boogeyman. I feed on the pain of them. Why does this surprise you Taura? You've always known I was a nightwalker."

"You could have spared me, you ass!"

"If they were seriously plaguing you, maybe I would. But until such a point in time I'm more than happy to be amused by them, you know he'd be hurt if he thought you were seriously upset."

"Yeah, I know," she grumbled, conceding his point ungraciously. "We all know a sulky Octavius is the worst."

Chuckling, I head over to the table to sift through the boxes. She wasn't kidding. An explosion of every color imaginable takes over the table. The joke must've extended to underwear and bras too, a mixture of bows, lace, and ruffles takes up two boxes, most of which are all different shades of pink... honestly, I adore it, and with Taura and I being a similar size I know I'd be able to find something.

CHAPTER 22
MEDUSA

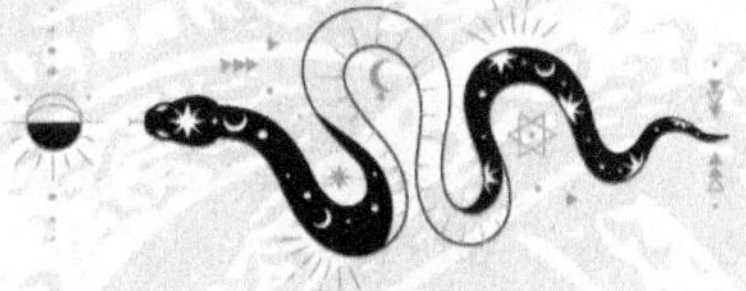

After a quick breakfast, Taura leads the way through the house out to a balcony and down the stairs I had spotted upon my arrival, we continue heading down until we reach the beach. As soon as my feet hit the sand, I feel all the tension in my body fade away, the black sand grounding me. The same cove that I had washed up on looks completely serene, as the water laps the sand in calm with gentle waves. Crystal clear water calling out for me to come closer. Smiling, I abide until I'm ankle deep in the water, looking out towards the horizon.

I notice two large Hippocampus covered in blue and silver scales sparkling in the sunlight. Jumping out of the water before diving back below they continue their play ignoring their mother who waits along with the rest of the group. Soon they concede before disappearing under the water.

"Such playful creatures, aren't they?" a familiar voice says from next to me. Octavius, I think his name is.

"Yes, they are," I reply as I turn my head, I take in his profile, his skin a golden bronze that one could only get from time spent in the sun. His long hair is pulled back in a low ponytail showing off his high cheekbones. My eyes seem to trail down taking in the shirtless man's face. I notice a trail of runes starting at his neck, I follow the wave-like designs down his arm and side till they dip below the waist of his shorts only reappearing at his knee and down his calf.

"Medusa, get that dress off and join me in the water, I need some girl time." Taura shouts from out in the water. Turning to see where Taura left her stuff, in my haste to dip my toes in the water I bypassed a large black canopy fitted with teal couches and wooden table.

"Where did this come from?" I say out loud forgetting that I wasn't alone.

"Taura likes to be comfortable on the beach, she says sand should not get in unmentionable places." Octavius answers me.

"Well after having sand in some of those places, I have to agree with her logic." I reply candidly before trudging over with Octavius by my side he settles in next to the other guys who have made themselves comfortable. Setting down the large towel I grabbed from the bathroom. Feeling a little self-conscious of my not super toned stomach amidst all these buff guys, facing away from the guys sliding the cute baby blue dress off, folding it up before setting it on top of my towel. I turn around after hearing a pained groan noticing a lull in conversation, looking around noticing seven sets of eyes on me.

"Is everything ok?" I ask, confused by the lack of conversation around me.

When no one replies I slide past Hades and Everett on my way to join Taura in the water, ignoring the not-so-subtle gazes I can feel burning holes into my back.

Instead of scurrying past like the meek mouse I used to

be, I channel my inner goddess. Adding a little extra sway to my hips knowing that these periwinkle cheeky bikini bottoms are displaying my asscheeks like the lady boss I am pretending to be. I am a strong-willed woman who doesn't care about the group of delicious monsters on the beach, nope not at all, I most definitely don't. And to prove how much I am unfazed by all the extra attention, I glide into the water like I own it. When the water hits my waist I murmur to my hair, "Hold your breath," before diving into the water.

Instantly the cool water is like a balm to my soul, I needed this. I stay beneath the waves for a moment, opening my eyes to smile as I see a variety of fish and creatures swimming around, some playful while others swim in groups or schools. It's so peaceful and I wish I could stay down here forever, life seems a lot less complicated here then the surface world.

Soon my lungs start to burn, and I swim up towards the surface, the moment my head is free from the water I take in a few deep breaths before turning to float on my back, closing my eyes enjoying the water's soothing rhythm just a little longer before making my way over to Taura.

CHAPTER 23
OCTAVIUS

"Sweet baby krakens, she's wearing the cheekys?" I groan to Everett, unable to take my eyes off of the luscious, biteable globes of her ass. I remember buying those for Taura as a joke, and right now I think she got the last laugh. The sway in Medusa's step hypnotizes me, as I watch the twin beauties that are her buttcheeks sink into the water. "I think I just came a little... Everett, check my pants, I can't look away right now."

"Pull it together," he laughs, startling me with a hard smack to my ass. A spark of mischievousness hits me as I watch Medusa float across the top of the water. Taking a long swig of my spiced rum, I slowly raise the water around her just enough for her to not feel the splash of me diving beneath the water around her.

"What are you up to?" Everett whispers in my ear.

"You'll see." I answer back, shoving my bottle into his hand.

"Octavius," Everett growls, brushing off his warning. I give him a flirtatious wink before diving in and disappearing beneath the water, slowly releasing my hold on the water around Medusa, her body swaying just a little as the water flattens out. Swimming so that I'm fifteen feet down, I move till I'm settled right below my target.

With a command of my magic, I am shooting up towards the surface. Every second I get closer with a speed that even a siren dreams they could possess, the water pushing me like a shooting star up towards Medusa and hurling us above the water like a pair of hippocampus's that we saw playing earlier in the water. Wrapping my arms around her as we both scream- her with surprise and me with laughter, I yell, "hold your breath."

"What the fuck!!!" Medusa screams just before we both drop back into the water. When we pop back up Medusa is sputtering, when she finally catches her breath, she pushes away from. "What the hell was that for?"

"I'm sorry Medusa I was just trying to make this beach day a little more fun."

"You call that fun?"

"Yes." I answer honestly to the tiny goddess while gliding closer to her. I can't help it. I want to know everything about her. She's an adorable little cinnamon roll I just want to devour. Wow that thought came out of nowhere. Pausing my pursuit of Medusa, she glides with ease away from me. My creature and I continue to track her movements while we try to sort out our true feelings over this woman.

"You, okay?"

I was pondering my thoughts that hadn't even noticed Medusa had moved closer till her tiny hand touched my skin sending a plunder of butterflies soaring through my insides.

"Aarrr!"

"Did you just say aarrr?" Medusa asks before bursting

into a full belly laugh. I swim closer to her worried she'll drown herself. Waiting till she calms down, my beast rumbles with joy of having her so close. The codfish is such a sucker for a pretty face.

"Who's a codfish?" Medusa asks curiously.

"Did I just say that out loud?"

"Yes, you did." Taura says as she swims between me and Medusa. Something neither my Kraken nor I like very much but I hold my tongue. I'm completely unsure as to why I truly dislike the space that is now between us. To top it off a three headed beast has appeared out of nowhere and is now taking off with Medusa. One of his heads has gently grabbed her wrist while he pulls her back towards shore.

"I believe you are being rescued." Taura teases as she swims beside Medusa and the dog.

"Oh, this good boy is definitely saving me from all those codfish," Medusa replies as she softly kicks her legs to help.

Cheeky woman. The moment they reach the shallow waters he lets go of her. The dog and Medusa sit in the chest deep water staring at one another.

"Hold on, I've got a few balls up at the house." Taura says just as she opens a portal and disappears. Smiling, I shake my head before swimming closer to Medusa, turning my attention back to the stray dog. I swear he looks familiar, but I can't place where I have seen him before. Reaching out I scratch his head closest to me.

"What are we going to do with you?" I ask the sweet beast.

"That is interesting. I've never met a creature I couldn't speak to." Medusa mutters. He whines and gives Medusa a sloppy, wet, three headed kiss, just before Taura appears next to us.

"Look what I've got beasty," she says as she shows the

dog a ball before throwing it across the beach. With an excited bark he races off towards the ball. His movements remind me so much of a manta-ray except on land instead of the ocean. It's kind of adorable to witness.

"Do I want to know why you have dog toys?" Medusa asks her.

"They're not mine! I took it from Kyrell's room." she tells Medusa, with a mischievously dark chuckle.

I burst out laughing. "He is going to be so pissed when he realizes," I say adding to the now raucous laughter.

"Food is ready," Everett yells at us from the beach just before he gets tackled by the dog.

"Whose dog is this?" Hades asks with curiosity as he strolls over to us from where he was walking alongside Everett. Stopping in his tracks when the giant three headed dog bounces over to him in turn licking him copiously and coating him in doggy drool.

"He's a stray," Medusa replies as we head towards the canopy.

"He's a stray? How did he make it past the wards? Is everything being welcomed in?" Hades shouts, stalking away in frustration, grumbling, and muttering to himself as he goes. Man, Hades really needs to chill out, or the grumpy bastard should double check how he commanded his wards to work.

Medusa storms ahead of me with Taura at her side. Damn it, Hades! He's such a fun spoiler sometimes. All conversation is lost as I bite the inside of my cheek as Medusa's biteable globes are back on display. My beast fights me wanting to place our mark on them. As we stroll behind her, I have to hold in a groan, my eyes feasting up the sight of her hips swaying. When we reach the others, I'm thankful she didn't notice my assessment of her assets.

CHAPTER 24
GAREN

While Medusa and Hades talk about the beast staying, Kyrell and I strategically decided we'd place Medusa between us. With Cooper right across from her. The pull we feel towards this woman seems to have grown overnight. If she is luring us in, we plan to stop it sooner rather than later.

Even with her stating last night she wasn't intentionally alluring us to her, the strength of the pull we felt was almost impossible to ignore. Hades though seems to be hellbent that is the case, he won't even take anything else we've suggested, even stating that the fates wouldn't be kind enough to give us a rare gift such as our center.

"Medusa you must try the salad. It's delicious with the roasted chicken." Taura says as she leans over my plate trying to hand the bowl over to Medusa. Grabbing the bowl of salad out of her grasp I set it back down on the table and dish up some onto a side plate for Medusa before adding some to my own.

"Thank you." the snake goddess next to me says before taking a bite out of the suggested food.

A comfortable silence falls over the table, only the clinking of silverware and the sounds of the waves can be heard. It's rather peaceful. Even with my soul pulling me to scoot closer to the woman next to me. Which I couldn't do even if I wanted to, as the three headed beast is laying between us, just as though it's a normal everyday thing they seem to do, while Medusa feeds him chicken from her plate. When she isn't looking, Kyrell or I sneakily add more chicken to her plate. She needs her strength, Kyrell and I will make sure she gets the sustenance she needs, regardless of her giving half her plate away to the pup.

"*I don't feel any magic being used.*" Cooper says through the bond.

"*Impossible, it has to be.*" Hades growls back.

"*Well, it seems like it's not entirely impossible, Hades. Maybe we should start looking into other ideas of why we feel so drawn to her.*" Kyrell adds calmly, using an answer that even Hades can't disagree with.

"*Fine.*" Hades relents. A sudden lightness struck my senses. I can feel everything is heading the way it was meant to be, even if I'm unsure what part Medusa is meant to play in our life, she has brought something back into our home we were missing.

"So, Medusa, what are some of the things you like doing?" I ask running a hand through my hair pushing back some pieces that had fallen into my eyes. Her purple gaze follows the movement, while she chews on her lower lip as she thinks over what she wants to say.

"I'm very simple, when I wasn't asked to help with a creature or someone's garden, I spent the days either reading, taking care of my home, riding. Some days I'd even go swimming in the pond by my house."

"I bet you lived close to my brother, since Hera surely had you help her. That garden of hers was always way too much for her to handle on her own." Hades stated while cutting a piece of his chicken.

Medusa set down her silverware, lifting her chin looking Hades in the eye, "Actually I lived in the Evercrest Forest, I'm sure you've heard of it."

Hades set down his own silverware, his arms overlapping, resting against his broad muscular chest. "I have, the damn forest hates my brother. He can't step foot into the place without it opening up to the mazes below."

"Hmmmm, interesting." Medusa says, posing a finger under her chin.

"It's true, Hera used to hide out there when he would piss her off. Which if you can imagine was hilarious. She didn't have to punish him, the forest did it for her." Hades added as his eyes glazed over.

"So, you were a real homebody?" Octavius teases.

"Sort of." she answers vaguely.

"Who is your favorite author?" Kyrell asks, before taking a bite of food.

Medusa's body thrummed with energy, "That's a loaded question, and honestly so hard to just choose one."

"I don't believe that there must be one author you are favoring at the moment," Kyrell says, his eyes crinkling up into a smile.

"I'll tell you mine if you tell me yours." Medusa says, with a challenging glint sparkling in her eye. A slow smile touches Kyrell's lips.

"Hitmen and Hexes series by Charlotte Brice she is a fae author from the summer fae court of Lucelence."

"I haven't read her work yet." Medusa responds, "I'll have to check out her work when I get my own place."

"You don't need to wait, you can borrow my copy," Kyrell offers. Medusa's breath hitches as she stares up at Kyrell.

"I'd love that." she gets out.

Well, well this day was getting more interesting by the minute I was excited to see how things went while we had this goddess here with us.

CHAPTER 25
MEDUSA

Yesterday was such a nice day, something changed between me and the guys, even Hades seemed to be a little less of a tightass. After eating me and Taura swam some more, Octavius helped me collect seashells. Kyrell kept asking me about the different books I've read, and I told him if he liked the fantasy books he should read Of Magic and Contempt by Jade Thorn, another famous fae author from the Eramnesia island.

"Here is the training room," Octavius says as he leans against the side of the door letting me and beasty see into the large space. The room is just as tall as the library down the hall but instead of shelves filled with books. A place I plan on returning to later tonight. The training room has one wall covered in an assortment of weapons. Off to our right is a place with floor mats that Kyrell and Ace are doing hand to hand combat. Both of the guys are moving incredibly fast yet with a grace that if one didn't know any better, they'd assume the two are dancing. Trying not to stare but it's so hard when all I want to do is lick the sweat off their abs.

"They do look delicious." Octavius says from next to me, causing my body to jerk back to reality.

Staring at my feet, I worked to steady my own breathing and my rush of hormones. Something that I was finding harder to control around the eye candy that filled every space of the house it seemed like. No matter what room Octavius showed me on this tour one of them joined us or were doing something tantalizing. Hell Hades was sitting in the library reading and all I could think about was how the chair he sat in could fit us both comfortably. My obsession with them all was not healthy.

"Enjoying the show snake goddess?" Ace asks as he and Kyrell walk towards us.

I feel a hot flush stain my cheeks, as I drink in the way they move, every step bringing them closer. I try to respond but the words are stuck in my throat, embarrassingly all I can do is stare as Ace walks right up to me.

"It's okay I don't mind you watching me. Maybe soon I can tempt you into joining us." I know he means for the training they were doing, but my thoughts can't stay clean. They all go straight to the gutter of rolling around on the ground with these guys.

"There you are Medusa," Taura says. Thank the fates Taura has perfect timing, "I talked to Hades, me and you are heading into town tomorrow. I'll show you around and we can also get you some clothes and other items of your own."

"Sounds perfect." I reply as I think about how I'll also be able to job search at the same time.

"We can discuss everything you need while we eat, Everett made lunch." Taura tells me as she links our arms together. Walking back down the hall with my new furry shadow we turn left and then head up the stairs for about three floors before we head down the hall to our right. The closer we get to the kitchen the more food I can smell.

"I hope you like it, I made potato soup, it's a favorite around here for rainy days." Everett says as he fills up bowls.

"I'm sure I will." I reply.

"It is the best thing you'll ever taste." Taura adds as she grabs a bowl filled with rolls. I grab a couple of the bowls and follow her into the dining room. The windows facing the cliff side make it seem like we are on the back side of a waterfall as a river of water glides down its smooth surface. I set the bowls down on the table before turning to head back and grab another, Taura's hand shoots out grasping at my arm. "Don't worry the other guys will grab the rest of the food, just sit and relax."

Nodding I take the seat next to her leaving only one open chair on my right. "I wonder who will get that chair."

"My guess is Octavius, he can be rather sneaky."

"I think Ace will grab it and either Kyrell or Hades will glare at him till he moves."

"I doubt Hades will sit there." I reply just before the guys walk in. Surprisingly, Everette sits down in the space next to me, Kyrell and Hades did glare at him, but he ignored them. After a little bit they sat down at the other end of the table since everyone else found their own seats.

"This is really good." I tell Everette before I take another sip of the soup.

"Thank you, it's an old family recipe." he replies. I humm my appreciation as I eat some more, Everett sets down a glass in front of me while I snagged a couple rolls setting them down on the small plate next to my bowl. Swallowing the food I scarfed into my mouth, I then take a big drink of what looks like fae wine. Taking a sip, I realize it's not, this stuff is delicious, the tanginess of oranges and spices mixed with something else tingles my senses.

"What is this?" I can't help but ask, it almost overtakes coffee for the title of Best Drink Ever.

"Stardust wine, it's from a special collection of a vineyard I own." Hades answers.

"Well, it tastes even better than fae wine. I think it's my new favorite wine." I reply with a genuinely warm smile.

"It was one of my favorites to create." Hades replies, smiling back at me as he pours himself another glass.

"I can see why." I respond before finishing off my own glass Everett is filling it back up before I even get a chance to ask. "Thank you, Everett."

"It's my pleasure amica mea."

CHAPTER 26
MEDUSA

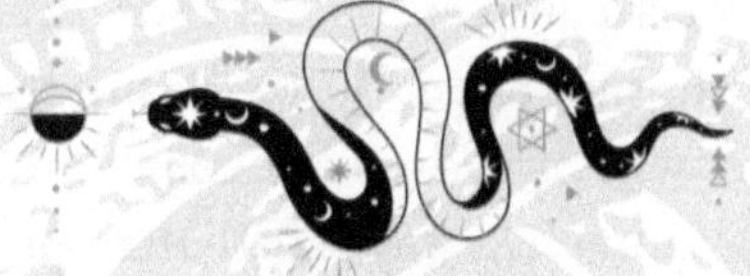

I refuse to give the gods the satisfaction of seeing this curse get the better of me. I will be stronger than this curse, I will become one with the creature within, and then one day when I am strong enough, I will get my revenge. That's what I keep telling myself as I slither over to the door, hearing Taura approach. Before she can knock, I fling open the door.

"So... I'm in a bit of a bind... I had a little freak-out"

"I'd say more like a snake-out...hahaha... get it? Snake-out, because you've got a snake body and..."

"Yep, got it," I cut Taura off before she could come up with more witty lines.

"You should have called for me sooner. Next time you snake out just holler." Taura says as she steps into the room before gently shutting the door behind her and settling on the ground next to me.

"I am so sorry about your clothes," I say as I turn to look at the pile of torn fabric.

She looks over as well, "Don't sweat it, they are just clothes." She tells me while standing back up in the blink of an eye. "I'll be right back." Taura says, before rushing out of my room.

I close my eyes as I sag against the couch, the heat from the flames warming and relaxing me. A sigh of contentment falls from my lips. For just a moment, I pretend that life is perfect and not a complete mess. That Atticus and I left Karpathos with Sumerian. I daydream that he's just a simple walk downstairs, drinking coffee and cooking food with Suma, bonding over my failed attempt at cooking the night before and agreeing I should be relieved of cooking duties for the foreseeable future.

My daydream is interrupted by Taura chucking a bundle of clothes at me.

"I brought you a skirt, I thought it was a safer option for you to wear for today. You know just in case you snake out. It shouldn't tear, and when you shift back you won't be naked." Taura tells me, placing the sandals on the floor sitting down across from me.

"Thank you," I tell her. Not sure how I'll ever be able to repay her or the guys for their kindness. Aside from Atticus and Sumerian no one has ever cared so much about me or helped me so much. Yet here Taura is sharing her clothes with me, about to take me to get my own things.

"It's no big deal," Taura says softly, pulling my hand into hers giving it a gentle squeeze as she smiles at me. "Okay, so I am going to teach you how to bring your legs back out," she says, both of us looking down at my tail.

I chuckle wiping a single tear off my cheek, "I think that would be a good idea before I leave the house." I reply thinking of how nice it would be to at least get my legs back.

"Alright, so the best way is to think about this like you are calling or recalling your powers. Only instead of plants, I want you to close your eyes and envision yourself with legs. Then hold that vision till you feel the change take hold and wash over you."

I nod before closing my eyes. I imagine myself with legs instead of a tail, I hold that vision of myself till I feel the tingling sensation that I felt when my tail appeared. I peek open one of my eyes. Thrilled to see my legs again. Just to double-check I wiggle my toes to make sure they are really back.

"I knew you could do it." Taura praises, "Now let's get you dressed and escape before one of the guys, or all of them, join us on our girls' day." She adds standing up, holding out a hand to help me up.

I quickly slip on the skirt followed by the sandals. Turning, I catch sight of myself in the mirror. I smile at my snakes coiling through the air. "I guess we look okay," I say to myself before braving my way over to the door and opening it.

"Don't worry, we will find you clothes that make you look and feel like the sexy-as-sin goddess you are," Taura says, linking our arms as we make our way down the stairs.

"I have no doubt about that," I reply with a smile, just as Taura rushes us over to a portal she created.

Stepping through together, we appear downtown. At least according to Taura.

"My shop is down that way, we will stop by there and get you all sorts of lotions and soaps for your bathroom. But first I need to fuel up, I hope you like coffee – because even if you don't, you will after you try some here." Taura says stopping in front of a shop. Looking up I read a sign that says, The Dirty Brew Cafe.

"Like? More accurately I am obsessed, it's my lifeblood." I answer passionately stepping inside.

Instantly getting in line. I move around, trying to see the

sign showing all the new drinks I can try. Sadly, the giant in front of me with his hoodie on is blocking the whole damn space.

With a sigh I stand there, Taura giving a knowing look. Taking mercy on me, she starts to tell me about some of her personal favorites.

In the middle of her discussing all the pros to choosing her favorite drink: Chocolagasam, I feel a whoosh of hot air on my neck. Whatever is behind me feels close to my height and smells like campfire smoke with a hint of ...wet dog?

I look over ready to give some creeper a piece of my mind and explain to him that there is such a thing as personal space. Instead, I come face to face with the biggest, wrinkliest, three-headed dog I've ever seen. And I am fairly positive that Taura and I had left said gorgeous, three headed dog behind with the guys today, he's just lucky he's so damn cute! A wide smile breaks out on my face, he is absolutely adorable, I just want to squish his cute faces. How did he track us here? The naughty thing, even if it is totally adorable and heart melting, that he followed us all the way here.

"Hi there, cutie," I say, as I scratch behind his ears of the middle head while the other two are licking at my face. "Aww, who's an adorable floof, you are. You're so cheeky, aren't you? Sneaking out like that! I know you're new to our little family like I am, but the others at home are probably worried sick about you boy. Oh well, you're here with us now aren't you boy. You be good and behave and I'll nag Everett to bake you treats when we get back" I coo.

Flopping onto his back, his tongue lolling out his three mouths leaving small puddles of drool, while waiting for me to scratch his belly. I happily oblige. Of course, I hadn't realized how close he was to others until his tail smacks the giant man knocking him out of the way.

"What the fuck?" I hear a deep-timbered voice growl.

"Sorry, I guess this sweet boy doesn't know his own tail strength. I-" I say starting to apologize but finding it difficult to form coherent words when our eyes meet. All I can do is stare.

Thankfully I wasn't the only one staring, his hazel eyes swirling with emotion taking in my small form. Using his own distraction to my advantage my eyes travel down his masculine nose that gives way to plump lips. I continue taking in his face with a strong jaw, and harsh angles but overall, his face was one that could make anyone's panties catch on fire. I continue to peruse this fine male specimen gazing down to his large chest and onto his tree trunks for legs, his gray sweatpants skin-tight leaving nothing to the imagination. Everything screamed ginormous about the man, his height hitting close to seven feet.

My snakes are helpless watching him with curiosity.

Taura bends down next to me, "I think he's staring because your ass is making an escape out of the skirt."

That seems to jolt us both out of our stare-off. Standing up I tug down my almost ridiculously short skirt. Why do they never give these things enough length to pass the sit and bend test?

"Sorry about this cutie pushing you. I am Medusa, by the way." I say holding my hand out for him. He smiles, encasing my hand in his.

"I am Othello, and it's no problem, Medusa, this big slobbering beast is with me. His name is Nero. He usually doesn't interact with customers... or anyone else for that matter." he tells me.

"What do you mean Nero is yours? He keeps randomly

popping up where I am staying, sleeping in my bed and then disappearing again? He found me on the beach with the others. I just assumed that I'd somehow collected him." I am still questioning if he's telling me the truth, as I tell him this. Because it's absolutely true! Even when you're asleep, you can't really miss a three headed dog climbing in next to you. Only to have him disappear before the sun comes up. And three headed dogs are extremely rare, so he would be the only one in this part of the country.

"Given he's my familiar and I have been wracking my brains trying to figure out where he's been creeping off too recently yeah, I'm positive he's mine. Lucky, traitorous bastard.... What's your poison ladies? How do you like your brew? Or would you prefer me to guess and surprise you?"

"Oh my gosh. I love surprises." Taura squeals, interrupting Othello. "I am Taura by the way, best friend of this beautiful creature," she announces, shocking me a little with her claim. Honestly, it feels right, and so nice to have a female friend who isn't an animal. With a secret wink at me he faces Taura.

"Well then, it would be rude for me not to deliver. You lovely ladies, just relax and I'll bring your drinks on over to you when they're done." Othello says.

"But we have to pay first," I reply, not sure how I feel about him surprising me with my coffee. I had high coffee standards for a reason and a Goddess even a cursed one like me should never compromise on standards.

"It's on the house. Now shoo, go make yourselves at home, while I get busy making these drinks." Othello says as he shuffles Taura and I over to a table with two sofas on either side of it. While Nero follows him over to our table, much to my surprise and his panty melting owners, he flumps down at the foot of my sofa and leaves all three heads sagging on my lap. Nero turns a deaf ear to Othello's calls and remains stubbornly situated with his heads in my lap. Thel as I think I'm going to call him, shrugs and walks away to get our drinks.

"Really?" looking into the eyes of each head as I gently scold Nero while I stroke the fur around his neck joins. "You couldn't have given me the heads up that you already have a super sexy familiar? And why if you have that to curl up next to at night do you keep sneaking into my bed with me? I might've had company you know," Nero huffs at that. "Well, I obviously know I didn't, but still, it's the principle of the thing." he huffs again which gives Taura the perfect opportunity to break in on our little tiff.

"Awwww it's so cute that you're conversing with all three heads. It's adorable, you may not have noticed but your snakes seem to like him." Her words leave me a little shocked. I notice that my snakes, who have been happily bouncing around my shoulders all morning, have lengthened significantly. Each and every one of them was now blissfully curled up on, or around Nero and his heads and all of them seemed blissfully content with that arrangement. I couldn't help but wonder if they curled around him like that unbeknownst to me while I slept.

"Here is a Chocolategasm for you and for Medusa I have our house specialty Liquid Life." Othello says and he hands me an actual coffee mug before he takes a seat next to me on the couch.

"Shouldn't you be working?" I ask him as I blow on my drink.

"One of the benefits of being the owner, I make my own schedule. Plus, my shift doesn't start for two more hours." He admits before taking a sip of his own mug. Sniffing the drink I'm hit with a delectable aroma, it reminds of a chia spice latte. A hint of pumpkin and cinnamon. A strange brew of delightful smells and blend of flavors I'd have never thought to mix together. "It tastes even better than it smells. And if you don't like it I'll make you something else till we find your drink." Othello promises.

"Deal." I tell him before I lift the mug to my lips and take a sip. My taste buds explode with flavor, Othello wasn't lying when he said it tasted even better. Honestly it is better than better it's orgasmic the way all the flavors and spices he has combined into this drink. Not to mention the energy buzz I've gotten just from one taste.

"Well does the drink pass?" Othello asks sincerely, the look on his face shows only a small bit of how unsure he is that he picked the right drink. His eyes sparkle with curiosity as he waits for my reassurance. Taking one more sip I let out a moan as somehow the flavor has gotten even more flavorful. A huge grin now graces his face. "I'll take that moan as a yes it has passed your taste test."

"It's more than passed; I will need a dozen of these to go." I tell him.

"I think we can work something out." Othello says with a wink. Dear fates all mighty, is it hot in here or did that drink awaken something else in me. Instead of fanning myself off like I want to I take another sip of my coffee while also giving Nero scratches.

"So should we call you the brew master?" Taura teases.

"I guess you could, my best friend Raiden and I create all the original and unique recipes for the coffee shop and The Bent Broom next door."

"What's the Bent Broom?" I ask while I sip more of my drink only to frown when I realize my cup is empty. Looking down at the mug I peek inside to see if maybe it's just a trick.

"Need a refill?" Othello chuckles as he stands up.

"Yes please." I reply as I hand him my mug.

"I'll be right back. Taura, do you need another one?"

"I'd love another one." She tells him as she hands him her glass.

Othello nods his head before heading back behind the counter, from where we are sitting, I can't see him do much, but with him being so tall I can see him look my way and give me a smile that makes my heart happy.

"So, I have a brilliant idea for tonight." Taura says drawing my attention from the coffee hunk.

"And what is this brilliant idea?" I ask truly curious as to what is going on in Taura's head that has a mischievous smile taking over her face.

"We go dancing, get out of that dusty cave fort. A girl's night to finish off our day."

"That actually sounds fun." I reply, knowing that it will also be a possibility that we will run into Othello.

"What sounds fun?" Othello asks as he sets our drinks down on the coffee table before reclaiming his spot next to me.

"Medusa and I are going to The Bent Broom tonight for a girl's night out." Taura says with a smirk before taking a sip.

"If you want, I can put your names down for a table in the VIP section." Othello offers.

"Yes!!" Taura shouts.

"Well then, it's settled. I'll put the reservations under Medusa." Othello tells us as he chuckles at Taura's bubbly enthusiasm.

"You're truly too kind." I tell him.

"No, I'm not. This is me making sure there's a definite chance that I can see you later." Othello says to me flirtatiously as he grabs my free hand in his. I'm surprised by his forwardness yet a part of me craves this, I'm drawn to him like Atticus and the others. This really can't be healthy to crave this many men. All of them are completely different and yet they all feel right for me.

CHAPTER 27
HADES

"You all look like a bunch of lured fish. Chasing after the first worm you've seen." I say chastising my bonded as they stalk Medusa from down the hall until her and Taura disappear through a portal.

As one they all turn to face me, surprisingly it's Octavius who gives me the worst death stare I've ever seen. I adjust my legs as he stalks towards me.

"She isn't a trap, Hades. I've thought about what you said. This is the first time since meeting all of you that I really found a woman I wanted to be mine. It's no secret I've fucked women and men alike. Before I met you bunch that's all it was, fucking. A way to get my pent-up energy out. Now, I still like fucking, but it's different with all of you, and I imagine it will be with Medusa."

"I agree with Octavius, she feels like more." Everett adds.

"You all feel this way?" I ask the rest of our bonded. I want to ensure that if she is ours, we all feel it, not just a few of us. If we all feel this way, it gives me confidence and assurance, in knowing and understanding my own feelings towards the enchantingly beautiful goddess. She seems so perfect, as though she was made for us.

"My creature has been restless since he first scented her." Kyrell says.

"She is definitely not here to hurt us." Cooper adds, "I've felt no luring spells cast, I even had Taura add a blocker against anything that would make us think she is ours in her tea the other night."

"Are you going to admit you like her?" Kyrell teases. I glare at him, before looking at the others. With a sigh, I grumble and resign myself to the possibility that what my mates and I feel for her isn't a trap. Maybe she really is our center, only time and giving her a chance will tell.

"Fine, we'll see where this goes." I tell them.

"Perfect, now that that is settled, Ace and I are going to make sure she gets everything and more that she'll need." Octavius tells us before the two disappear into the shadows.

"We're on our way out, do you need anything from town?" Cooper asks as he stands by the front door with Everett, Garen and Kyrell.

"Actually, I do, give me a moment and I'll head into town with you guys." I say before rushing downstairs. When I make my reappearance into the room, my four bonded are waiting and all turn at once as if rehearsed. Their faces light up with smirks.

"What are you looking at?" I growl at them. The smug bastards!

"So did you dress up for us or are you trying to impress Medusa?" Everett asks as he bites his lip as his eyes travel up my body.

"I'm not dressed up," I growl out, even though I kind of am. I may not be sure what I feel for Medusa yet, but I want her to want me as much as she wants the rest of my bonded.

"Let's go make sure Octavius doesn't buy out the whole town." I add pulling open the door and stepping out. Smiling when I see a portal open right in front of me, Cooper knows how much I detest making my way through our forest trail to the town. Mostly since we have a few strange plants with sharp teeth that love to chase me.

The moment I step out of the portal on the cobblestone street, I see Medusa and Taura head into the coffee shop. Before I even get a chance to follow them the guys are dragging me towards their restaurant. I knew they had to get things opened and prepped but I didn't think I'd be more interested in stalking her. But I was.

How in the world did she get so deeply embedded into my mind, all I've been craving from the women is a chance to punish her and fuck her and claim her.

See.

Fuck I need to decide what I want from this goddess before I do something rash, like chaining her to my headboard and tasting every inch of her.

CHAPTER 28
OTHELLO

Medusa waves goodbye, before walking off as her friend says something about clothes and no more ass-showing to sexy strangers.

I smile, watching them disappear down the street into a store before Nero and I make our way across the street to the Poison Apple Apartments, where we live.

It was a thousand times nicer than any of the other places within my budget range. The large upscale building boasted spectacular views and magical rooms that fit each tenants' specifications. That is one thing I love about Zakynthos. Most other towns favored their own kind and the rest of us would have to make do, here every kind of supernatural is welcomed. The Poison Apple apartments were one of the most welcoming, they mix the different magics to make this place enchantedly one of a kind. No need for housekeeping when your room cleans itself, no need to make noise complaints when everything is magically sound-proofed, an absolute MUST when I am tired after a long day at work and all I want to do is pass out and get a few hours of sleep in before I head back to the grindstone.

"Welcome back, Mr. Othello." Eden the doorman says as he opens the door for me.

"Good morning, Eden," I reply back. I could have laughed at the shock on his face, the man had grown used to me just grunting out a hello.

"Nero, what has Medusa done to me?" I ask the beast walking next to me heading to the elevator taking us to the penthouse suite on floor thirteen.

It was a giant suite with a balcony and kitchen, living room, a master suite, and eight additional rooms – each with its own bathroom. It seems a bit excessive when there are only a couple people living in it, but I like my space and I have most of the guest rooms set up as brewing stations for when I am mixing new brews.

The penthouse was decorated like the rest of this place, with dark colors and various jewel-colored pieces furniture with hints of wood finishes and plants that seemed to take over some of the wall space features that I found soothing. Nero seemed to like the space too.

"Othello, is that you?" I hear my mate Raiden call out. He was one of the few people who I trusted to help me make the brews. Our taste pallet was similar, and he always seemed to know just what to add to make a new type of brew taste complete.

"I got coffee, and Nero was the best wingman today," I say as he casually strolls into the room. He smirks at me, knowing I don't usually care about hookups, but Medusa already feels like so much more.

"Tell me more about this new friend?" He says sitting on a stool at the counter.

"There isn't much to say, but I did only just meet her.

But Nero seemed to like her, in fact he seems to be far better acquainted with her than he should be, he was with her when he disappeared yesterday."

"Well then, she must be a keeper, to get past Nero, he's usually the cock block not the wingman. I can't wait to meet this mysterious woman." He says, jumping up from his stool. "I'm headed out for a run, I'll be back later, and you can tell me more about this woman. You got about ten minutes left before the new roast is ready for your magic life mojo, so you might want to take shower babe. You stink!" He adds with a laugh, before heading out the front door.

I lift my arm, taking a sniff, instant regret hits me. "Nero, why didn't you tell me I stink?" I ask the three-headed beast who is sitting wagging his tail. I dig in the cupboard for three bones, throwing them across the room before making my way into the master suite.

Thoughts of Medusa run through my mind while stripping out of my clothes, I was so close to rushing down the street and claiming her pouty lips. I wanted to taste and see if she was as sweet as her scent.

This must be my lucky day, for the fates led me to Medusa. It was more than an instant attraction I felt for her, it was an overwhelming need to claim her as mine just as I had with Raiden. To protect her and cherish her. My feelings for this woman are all consuming, all I can picture in my mind is her lying in bed between me and Raiden.

She tempts me like no other has, all the women who came before I met her are now being stripped from my memories. I know in my heart she will be the only one for us now.

CHAPTER 29
MEDUSA

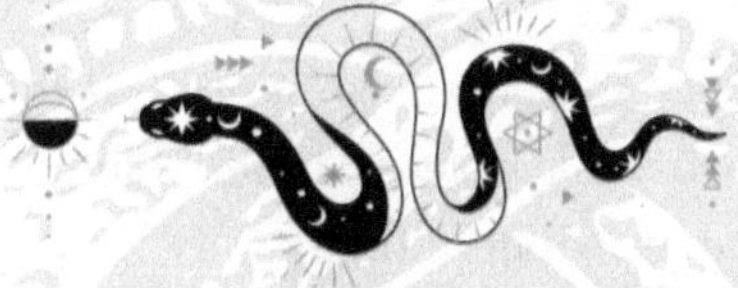

"Here, you need this, and this, and this. Oh, and this." Taura says, piling clothes into my arms. "Now go try them on so we can make sure we have the correct sizes." She says waving me off before taking a seat on the lounge. I do as I am told and head into the stall with the tower of clothing. I set them down on the bench before quickly stripping out of my borrowed clothes.

Looking over the large pile, I pick up a long flowy black skirt from the pile and pair it with a lacy top. Sliding the combo on, I smile when I notice pockets on the skirt. Without looking in the mirror, I step out of the stall to show Taura, getting ready to show off my snack holders. Only Taura is no longer alone, seven other figures are now sitting or standing around where I left her. The slight pout on her face tells me she isn't happy about our surprise guests.

"What are all of you doing here?" I ask, stepping closer to the group while crossing my arms. Taura stands up next to me, copying my pose.

"Yes brothers, why don't you tell her why you've all decided to drop in and spoil our girl's day." She says to them a smirk gracing her lips. They all look at each other before Hades makes his way over to us from where he stood on the other side of the lounge.

"We just so happened to be out and about, and running a few errands. Octavius realized he needed a tie." Hades says matter of factly.

"It was by chance that we happened to stroll by when we saw you two walk in and figured Medusa might need a little assistance." Cooper added.

"Oh really..." Taura says, narrowing her eyes at each one of them, "and why is that?"

"Well, we just wanted to make sure she was finding the clothes she likes and not the clothes you're forcing on her." Cooper says blatantly.

Taura stood there for a moment in shock, her face suddenly emptying of emotion except her eyes. Swirling vortexes of pitch black locked onto the guys, the only indicator she was getting ready to lose her shit. Feeling the need to intervene before Cooper made his way unexpectedly through the river of souls in Hell, I stepped between the two feuding siblings hoping to de-escalate the situation. "I actually love Taura's sense of style, she's really helped me pick through clothes. You just so happened to come right as I was getting ready to try some things on."

Hades steps closer to me, probably thinking that he's going to have to save me if the siblings get out of hand. An electric current buzzing between us making those damn butterflies in my stomach start to flutter around again.

"Why not just buy it all?" Hades asks. I arch an eyebrow at him in surprise and curiosity.

"I didn't want to waste your money on things I wouldn't wear." The side of Hades mouth quirks upwards just as Octavius struts on over.

"Well love, since we are here. Why don't you give us a show and let's see what you two have picked out." He says with a wink as he guides Hades over to the couch with him. When he sees I haven't moved an inch he waves his hand in a shooing motion before settling down with the others.

Glancing over at Taura I see she's calmed down and is lounging in a plush cushioned seat, thank goddess. She smiles and winks at me before shooing me to try on more of the outfits we picked. Not wanting them all to start a war while waiting for me, I walk back into the dressing room.

Slipping off the flowy skirt and lacy top. I then grab a black sundress that is at the from the rack in my dressing room. Slipping it on I glance down at it, the dress has thin straps and is soft as rose petals. I pull the curtain aside and screech as Taura is standing right on the other side. Taura grabs my shoulders pushing me back into the room closing the curtain behind us with magic.

"Don't head out yet. Octavius and Ace are grabbing you a few more things. Apparently, the Kraken thinks you need accessories as well as clothes." She adds just moments before both men enter with their arms full of more clothes, hats, boots, and belts.

Octavius blows hair out of his face before his gaze meets mine. His lips turning up into a smile as he sets down his pile on the bench. "If you allow me, I have a few things to add that I have a feeling will make this dress more you."

CHAPTER 30
OCTAVIUS

Smiling to myself as I watch Medusa's face go from normal to surprise by my request.

Okay, so maybe I'm not doing this right, but I couldn't help it. Even with Taura's help with finding clothes. I can already tell that Medusa would only accept the bare minimum of things she needs. Just enough to get by till she had her own money. She seems to be the type of person who has a hard time accepting help. I wait for her to say anything, when I see the small nod she gives me, I know she is okay with me adding a few small touches to her outfit.

I'm now grateful I let Ace talk me into watching from the shadows with him as I turn my back to her for a moment, grabbing the items I picked out specifically for this dress she is wearing. The clothing she has on is just a simple dress by itself, but with adding a few items it will enhance her natural beauty. I hand the black hat with the wide brim to Taura. Taking the belt in my hand, I bring Medusa close to me, cinching the belt around her waist.

"This buckle has a special catch on the side and a charm that allows the wearer to store and keep knives hidden."

Unable to help myself from smoothing down the fabric at her hips. Mesmerized by her full curves a throat clears behind me, glancing up at Medusa I see she is just as affected, a delicate rose staining her cheeks her pupils dilated. Breaking her stare, I pull the soft leather ankle boots from off the floor and kneel down.

Turning back to Medusa, I freeze while watching her glance down at the clasp and she finally notices the octopus shaped buckle. Her fingers caressing the tentacles, a smile spreading over her mouth.

"I figured you'd take good care of my ass." Medusa teases.

I wink at her before placing a boot on my knee. "Here, these should fit your feet." Medusa doesn't move. Instead, she looks over at Taura who has the same surprised look on her face. A chuckle slips out, snagging both their attention, "Is it truly surprising that I kneel before you?" I ask Medusa, while I hear Taura snicker.

She places her arms across her chest while swaying a bit. "Yes! I'm not the kind of goddess that was worshiped. So, you kneeling to help me put on a shoe is not what I expected you to do." She replies while looking at me from under long lashes. I'm absolutely dumbfounded at what she has said, obviously, the gods didn't know what they had within their world. If I was being honest, I'm glad they didn't, then she would never have splashed into ours.

"Well, it's a good thing you are no longer just a goddess then." While sending a silent vow to Medusa that I will spend every day worshiping her. I hold out my hand to steady her as she balances on one foot while sliding on the boot. "Now, just so you know, I've already paid for all these items, the boots are created with magic so they will never get ruined," I tell her.

"Thank you," she says so low it is a whisper. "But you shouldn't have, they must have cost a fortune. I'll pay you back." Placing two fingers under her chin, I lift her face till our eyes met.

"There is no need to pay me back, they are a gift from me to you."

MEDUSA

After my fashion show, most of the guys went back to work, all except Octavius who stayed with us as Taura dragged me from shop to shop. He carried most of the bags and even offered fashion advice when I couldn't decide between a few outfits. Okay, so his advice wasn't really advice but more statements, always complimentary and ending with "charge them to my card."

I'm positive I have enough clothes now to dress a whole forest full of creatures and accessorize them too.

"Okay, are you ready to see my shop?" Taura asks as she walks backwards facing me.

"Of course," I say, feeling like I might need another coffee with seven espressos. Who knew shopping could take so much out of you?

"Don't worry, I have an energy potion at my store with your name on it." She says as she winks at me. We continue walking when a delicious smell of fresh french fries hits me like a herd of Aequillas. Sniffing the air, I let the smell guide me till I'm standing out front of a diner.

"The Juniper Beetle." I read the sign out loud.

"Are you hungry, love?" Octavius asks.

"Starving," I reply as I pull open the door and enter, not even waiting for Octavius or Taura to say anything. My mind now was completely focused on getting food in my stomach.

I pitied anyone who got in my way. A tall woman stands before me. Her skin is an ashen color and reminds me of tree bark. Her green locks look like they have sticks and leaves woven into them, but it's her bright neon yellow eyes that pique my interest the most.

"Hi, welcome to the Juniper Beetle. How many people are in your party?" Octavius steps up, throwing his arm around my shoulders.

"Three today, Callie, and give us the big booth in the back corner." She smiles, showing off rows of sharp teeth.

"So, your regular spot, Mr. Vanora."

"Yes, and can you send out Cooper," Octavius says as he leads me over to the booth with Taura trailing behind.

"Cooper works here?" I ask.

"No, he owns the place with Everett and Garen," Taura replies.

I take in the restaurant, it's like nothing I've seen, the color scheme of this place reminds me of the several places we've been in town today. Zakynthos is the complete opposite of Karpathos; the buildings look to be as if they were plucked from an ancient village from the time of the ancients mixed with dark overtones.

It's all beautiful, in a gothic bohemian way with a dash of magic.

My eyes scan the room. All the walls are made of the same dark stone as the house with green accents. This place is a mixture of a diner and a gothic dream. The floor is covered in black onyx tiles, the booths are solid black leather, the tables, chairs, and barstools are all in a deep green. It is decorated lightly with black and white pictures of the years it has been here. There is one behind Taura that has all the guys in it, Cooper is holding a pair of scissors ready to cut the ribbon. While a banner behind them reads 'Grand Opening'. A menu is placed down in front of me.

"Thank you." I say to the waitress.

"You're welcome, Medusa." I tear my eyes from the picture to see Cooper smiling down at me.

CHAPTER 32
COOPER

Two jewel-like eyes look up at me, framed with long sweeping eyelashes that ensnare me in their gaze anytime I look at this enchantress.

"Mind if I sit?" I ask Medusa as I wait for her permission.

"Of course," she says as she scoots over towards Octavius.

"So how is the shopping going?" I ask slipping in next to her.

"This one here thinks I need everything in the stores." She says, gesturing over at Octavius with her hand. Octavius clutches his chest.

"You wound me with such words." He says as he falls back against the seat dramatically. I roll my eyes at his crazy antics. Peaking one eye open Octavius shifts forward, cupping Medusa's face, "A beautiful woman like you should have everything she desires and more." He tells her. She closes her eyes, taking a deep breath.

"What if what I desire is more than I can handle?"

"Then we will be patient and take it however slow or

fast you say." Octavius replies with such a ferocity that even I'm surprised.

Medusa's stomach rumbles ruin the sweet moment. "Sounds like first what you need is food. What would you like to eat?"

"Surprise me, but make sure it has a little bit of a kick to it. Oh, and fries," she replies.

I nod as internally think of what I could make for her before turning my attention over to Taura. "Just bring me my usual." my sister replies.

"You already know what I want, mate," Octavius says as he looks longingly over at Medusa.

"I'll be back with your food," I reply as I head back to the kitchen. No surprise the moment I enter, Eve and Garen are there, glaring at me. I chuckle at the sight of the two of them strapped up to the wall with my magic.

"Can you please release us now, Coop?" Garen asks nicely, while Eve is growling at me.

"Oh, come on Eve, I thought you both loved it when I tied you up," I say with a smirk.

"Not when I can smell our Medusa's scent on you." He grumbles. I lift my shirt up to my nose, sniffing it alone makes me moan.

"God, I'm never washing this shirt again." I groan. "You want a sniff?" I ask them.

"Shut up and undo our bindings. We have food to cook." Eve growls.

"Fine," I say with a snap of my fingers releasing the two. No surprise they both head out to see the snake goddess. I chuckle as I start cooking using my magic to help prepare the food. I also prepare a chocolate milk shake for Medusa.

"Eve get your ass back in here." I shout through our bond.

"One second Garen is telling Medusa a story."

I shake my head at the two. Without missing a beat, I snap my fingers finishing up the food and placing it on trays. I grab Medusa's milk shake with the floating trays of food following and head back out to feed my bonded, a snake goddess and my sister. I hold in a chuckle when I see Taura magically move Medusa to her side.

"You two are supposed to be working. Now go get Medusa's food, my girl is ravenous." She chastises Eve and Garen.

Eve is the first to get up and with a supernatural speed has Medusa up in his arms in a crushing hug whispering something in her ear that makes her blush. Garen is instantly right there stealing her from the gargoyle and then surprises all of us when he places a kiss on her lips. I stand frozen watching the kiss go from sweet to passionate. Octavius makes his way to my side.

"And you all thought I'd be the first one to kiss her," his voice low, so it only reaches my ears.

We did. Honestly, it's in his nature to push boundaries. Garen is one of the more levelheaded of our group, always thinking things through his usual reserved nature gone, a surprise I enjoy witnessing.

"Think we can get rid of the other customers and have our wicked way with her?" I ask through our bond.

"She's not ready for that." Octavius replies. Well fuck who are these men. Did they somehow switch bodies because for once Octavius is being well not Octavius. Finally, Medusa pulls her lips away from Garen's, their heads still bowed close as they stare at each other breathing heavily.

"Well, if you two are done our food has arrived and I'd like to eat before it gets cold." Taura says breaking whatever magical spell was happening between them. Garen glares at my sister but releases Medusa and allows her to return back to the table. Once she is settled, I set down her chocolate milk shake along with her food. She looks up at me, gracing me with a smile.

"This looks delicious. Thank you, Coop."

"It was my pleasure. Feel free to ask for anything else you want. We will be in the kitchen. And Octavius, make sure you two come say goodbye before you leave." I add before dragging the two other lovesick monsters with me.

"*So does she taste as sweet as she smells?*" Everett asks Garen.

"*Better.*" He says with a dreamy sigh.

I arch a brow at him. "*Are you sure you're not Octavius in Garens body?*" That seems to get his feathers nicely ruffled.

"*Yes. She is just so... so irresistible.*" And I can't argue with the truth of that.

"*That she is.*" I agree.

CHAPTER 33

MEDUSA

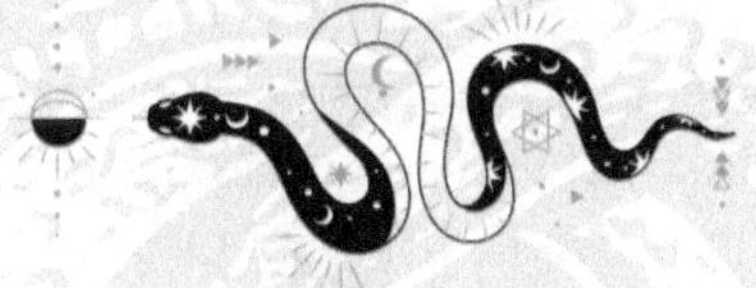

The fire from Garen's kiss has lit an inferno within, the warm tingling sensation traveling from my lips to other parts of my body, feeling worked up for something more. The frozen milkshake is unable to cool me down, my inner creature begging me to paint the leftover whipped cream all over Garen's body and feast. It's hard for me to reconcile this new bold being that I've become with the one I used to be. Yet I feel horrible for feeling this way when my heart first belongs to Atticus.

If Atticus was here, would he even recognize me? Would he still feel the way he said he felt before we left for Hera's party? I know my feelings for him haven't changed but what about him? I instantly feel guilty and self-conscious. The monster inside of me needing more and finding no fault with the idea of caring for multiple partners. At this point, I don't know if I will ever see him again, I have no idea what my future holds.

"Are you okay? You went from hot and bothered to pensive." I hear Taura ask me.

"Yeah, I just feel like I am going through all these different changes and feelings that I don't know who I really am anymore. Before I showed up on these shores, I left behind someone I really loved who I thought I would be with forever. I am trying to not feel so guilty about developing an attraction to others. The creature side of me is craving something I never thought possible, and I am struggling a little bit with accepting this new side of me." I admit, just a little nervous of what Octavius and the others would think. Surprisingly Octavius smiles softly, placing a warm hand on mine.

"Well maybe you should just see where everything goes. It's possible it could lead you to something incredible."

"And if it doesn't?" I ask, hoping Octavius has something more to say that will cure my thoughts that keep telling me this won't work.

"Then I'll curse them." Taura says with a wink. "Are you done eating?"

"Yes, let me say bye to the guys and we can go to the next store." I reply, sliding out of the booth. I feel Octavius close behind me. I make it to the kitchen door suddenly feeling unsure about all of this. I'm nervous about the progression of my feelings for these guys.

"Does the mate bond always make you feel so intensely about each other?" I softly ask Octavius.

"I'm not sure, I can only really speak for myself and the feelings I get through our bond. For me, having them in my life feels like home and a sense of belonging. Prior to that I felt a restless sense of energy, never feeling like I could stay in place for too long. My beast is a sea dwelling creature, most content and at home in water. For me, the bond feels the way I feel about water: complete and at peace. The restlessness I used to feel when away from the water is gone and replaced by a sense of belonging that I'd been missing. Until one day I found a very pissed off God who was mad I stole his crown and got him wet. Between you and me I didn't want to get burned so I had no other choice but to douse out his blue flaming hair."

I feel a smile tug at my lips as I picture a soaking wet Hades scolding a carefree Octavius.

"What happened after that?" I ask, wanting to learn everything about these men.

"I shifted back and with my natural charming self I fucked him till he couldn't remember anything else." I twist my head to meet his gaze. "Don't worry love, I'll wait for you to command me to fuck you. I can wait for that sweet treasure of yours." He says his lips grazing mine. Before he struts forward pushing open the swinging door and heading into the kitchen. I rush in after him, feeling like a string connected to my heart and soul is pulling me to them.

I stop up short when I see all four of them standing together smiling and waiting for me.

"See I told you all she was coming to say goodbye." Octavius says to the others.

Everett holds open his arms and I waste no time stepping into his embrace. I feel even more tiny in his arms. The man is a giant, but to be honest they all are. And I wasn't a very tall person to start with. Everett places his nose between my shoulder and neck taking a deep breath in. Instantly a rumbling sound vibrates from within him.

"My gargoyle wants to keep you in our arms forever." He whispers into my neck.

"Protective much." I hear one of the others mutter.

"Maybe one day." I reply not sure what else to say to

that. With one last sniff Everett reluctantly sets me down just in time for another pair of iron bands to pick me up. The smell of mocha, leather and magic hit my senses and I knew that Cooper had grabbed me before Garen could.

"Stay safe." He whispers in my ear. I nod before he releases me. My feet don't even touch the ground before Garen snags me.

"Mine." He chirps out before his lips are back on mine.

"That's twice he's kissed her." I hear Octavius shout causing Garen to chuckle.

"Be careful, beautiful and we'll see you at home." Garen says still holding me captive.

"I will." I promise him.

"Garen let her go, we've got some lingerie shopping to do. And I for one am looking forward to this show." Octavius says, making both of us turn to look over at him.

"Change in plans Octavius stays here with us, you and Taura go have fun. No fashion shows." Everett says as he ushers me out of the kitchen while Cooper holds Octavius back. Or at least he tries to, but the sneaky shifter slides out of his grasp and instantly has his arm over my shoulder as we walk out of the kitchen.

"Time to go to Taura." Octavius says as he grabs her arm dragging her away from the male she was talking with. Taura looks over at me with a what the fuck look? I just smile and shrug my shoulders.

As Octavius leads us to the next store. Apparently, he was not joking about the lingerie shop. And no surprise he is buying everything for me. Thankfully he doesn't want me to model the items for him here. But does say a private show will be requested at a later date.

After the lingerie store Taura drags me to her shop a

few doors down she loads me up with everything a girl could need. She even adds a sparkly glass dildo into my bags saying that I'll for sure need it. At least until I'm ready to go there with any males.

CHAPTER 34
MEDUSA

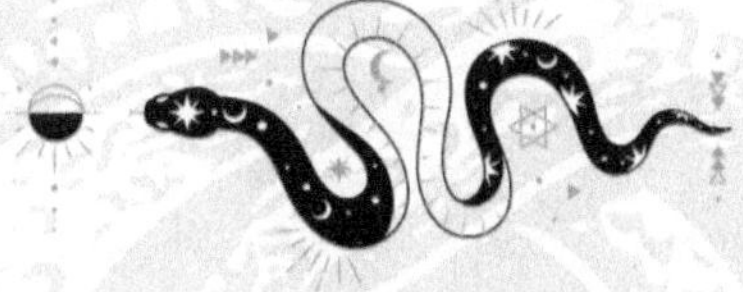

Stepping inside the doors. I'm thrown off as there only seems to be books. A few people sit around with drinks at a small bar tucked in the corner.

"Taura, I think we're a bit overdressed." I tell her, as I start to feel uncomfortable and a little sad. I was looking forward to some dancing and spending more time with Taura and maybe even seeing Othello.

"Relax Medusa, let's go get a drink." She tells me before heading right over to the bar.

"Hello beautiful ladies, what can I get you both tonight?" The bartender asks.

"We would like the blue spirit." Taura says.

"An excellent choice." he responds before sliding Taura two crystals on a long leather cord, the crystals themselves I recognize as Luminous.

"Don't lose this." Taura tells me as she hands me one before sliding hers over her head. Not wanting to lose this stone I do the same.

"Two blue spirits." The bartender tells us, gesturing to

our waiting drinks. Taura picks one up and nods before heading towards the wall of books.

"Thank you." I say as I grab my own glass and catch up to Taura.

"You ready?" Taura asks with a smile.

"Ready for what?"

"To have the night of your life." she says before pulling down a book.

The bookcase swings forward opening up into a hall filled with wisteria trees lining a pathway, these trees seem to be glowing lighting the way. Looking back over my shoulder I see no one else is paying attention to us. Linking our arms Taura drags me inside just before the door starts to creek as it slowly closes once more. My feet shuffle as I take in the beautiful and unique plants that surround us.

"I've never seen plants like this before." I tell Taura as I reach out, allowing my magic to interact with these plants.

"They originate from the underworld, but over the centuries they found their way up to the surface of our island." Taura explains just before we continue forward, even as the foliage slowly sparsest out. Soon it is dark with only soft blue lights glowing in the distance.

Stepping out of the forest hall, I realize we are standing on the second level. My jaw hits the floor. The place opens up into a cavernous room. From the ceiling that appears at least forty feet up are fairy strings intermingled with more glowing wisteria vines. The mixture of the two sends an aurora of colors across the room. Down below us I can see on the far wall a bar made of black stone and silver accents. A whole team of bartenders manning the drink orders. Behind the wall has shelves that go up till they sit just below the second floor, all filled with alcohol.

"Want to get a closer look?" a familiar voice asks me.

Turning so fast my head collides with Othello's.

"Are you okay?" I instantly ask him while my snakes grumble at me.

"I'm fine, my head is a lot harder than yours." He jokes.

"Good, now if you don't mind could you show us to our table?" Taura asks.

"Yes, but first let me buy you girls your next drinks for the night." Othello offers before offering us both an arm as we walk down the black metal spiral staircase. I smile as I notice the ornate vines and flowers made of metal that flow down the sides of the railing. Only to gasp when I finally notice the floor which looks to be a solid black stone with veins of blue luminous flowing sporadically through like a river. We weave through a sea of customers, and I catch a glimpse of the dance floor. In the back is a large stage with a band playing.

"You have live bands play?" Othello looks over at me.

"Yes, tonight we have several bands playing. In hopes we can find a few news ones to perform on rotation. That way every night isn't the same and allows everyone the choice of something different."

"That's absolutely brilliant." I reply.

Stepping up to the counter closer to Othello, I take a look at the drink menu. With so many options, I have no clue what to choose. Our close proximity and his general hotness melting what few brain cells I have left. It just feels right? I'm pretty sure I'm silently losing my mind with all the recent male hotness I've been surrounded by lately after my desert-like dry spell these past few years. Pretty sure my dry spell is up, and my body has just declared I'm in the wet season. Feeling my face heating, I try to turn my thoughts to safer ground. Focus on the drinks Dusa. Focus on the drinks.

"I have no clue where to start. There are so many options." I exclaim, as I still struggle to control my wayward thoughts.

"I'll take a creamy sex on the beach." Taura says to the bartender.

"That sounds good, can I get one of those as well." I say.

"Anything for you Bossman?" the bartender teases Othello.

"Not at the moment, Raiden."

"Raiden, isn't he your partner?" Taura asks Thel. A blush tinges Othello's cheeks.

"Yes." My eyes widen at his answer, as I look between them, guilt fills me. As my head keeps pin ponging between the two men. I feel vile and ill.

"I need to go." I hear myself say, I start to back up on auto pilot. Othello and Raiden both watch me as I keep backing up from them. I search the room for an exit on this level but can't seem to find one. Before I know it, Raiden is hoping over the bar and is now before me.

"It's okay Medusa. You didn't ruin anything; in fact, you are just adding more into our little family." Raiden says to me as he slowly pulls me in closer to him while Othello comes up to my side. I take in the two handsome giants, Othello and Raiden. "We like you Medusa." Raiden tells me.

"You don't even know me." I tell him as I look up into his ice green eyes.

"True I don't but I'd like to. We both would." Raiden answers confidently. The biggest issue is, how on earth am I meant to tell him they are not the only ones who feel this way.

"Are we interrupting something?" Closing my eyes, I let

out a groan. The fates really are testing me tonight. Opening my eyes, I look over to see Hades and the others.

"What on earth are you all doing here?" Taura asks her brothers.

"Octavius's band is performing tonight, and we thought we'd come support him." Cooper explains while I stand there having a mini panic attack. The pull I feel to all these men hits me tenfold. It takes a lot of focus to keep my body from shifting and wrapping them all in my tail, yet I don't know how to explain this to any of them without it sounding weird and possessive. My inner beast just hisses at me as she informs me in her own way that it's not weird to put a claim on the men who are ours.

Damn I need a drink.

"Which band is his?" I hear Raiden ask my other guys while he wraps an arm around my shoulders drawing me closer to his side. A move that doesn't go unnoticed by any of my men.

I mean the men, they're not mine.

"Eternal Voyage." Kyrell answers without taking his eyes off Raiden's arm.

"Perfect, now you all get to know each other. Medusa and I are going to enjoy our girl's night." Taura says as she hands her empty glass to Raiden and pulls me out of the meat circle. "Play nice brothers, they are crazy about Medusa as you all are." she adds as she pushes me in front of her to walk.

"Don't worry about them! They're grown men, they'll figure out how to make it all work." Taura tells me while latching our arms together and heading to the dance floor. The current musician is incredible, she sings and dances around the stage while playing a crystal energy violin that creates different sounds on her whim. Her melody's draw you in and take away your worries. Something I needed after the interaction with the guys.

Taura and I sway along to her sweet tones, closing my eyes I truly lose myself to the melody, that I forget that I'm even in a bar with others instead I'm back at my home in the Evercrest forest dancing in the field while the firefly's flutter around me.

"Your new booth is ready." Othello tells me as he pulls me into his arms.

"New booth?" I ask curiously.

"Yes, it's one of our bigger ones that can accommodate all of us."

I look over at Taura who is giving me a very 'I told you so look'.

"Lead the way." I tell Othello.

"It would be my pleasure."

I have a feeling this will be a night I won't ever forget.

CHAPTER 35
HADES

I watch as Othello leads Medusa back towards our booth. Our snake goddess just keeps bringing more and more surprises into our life. Like a hurricane, she swept in with no warning and has turned my carefully laid out life upside down. Dragging into the mix more bonded we never knew we were missing. When I look over at Raiden his aura screams a mixture of life and death just like Othello's.

While we allowed Medusa and Taura to dance without us, we talked. Othello and Raiden explained their uniqueness. Mates, they have been together for about as long as me and the others. Though Raiden had caught nightswish a sickness that kills any supernatural who isn't immortal.

It's a slow-going sickness that starts with making you tired a little more every day you grow weaker and more tired till you fall asleep never to wake again. Yet Othello couldn't let him go, he saved Raiden with a magical brew. And now they keep it at bay, Raiden once only a normal alchemist mage now a zombie.

"Move over you big lug." Taura says as she pushes on Cooper.

"Ask me nicely."

"Never," Taura replies before waving her hand making her brother float right out of his seat allowing her and Medusa to sit together before she sets him back on the bench.

"What can I get you all to drink?" a waitress asks as she stands at the end of our table.

"Start us off with the blue potion specialty shots." Raiden tells the waitress.

"Do you have a menu?" Medusa asks as she leans forward so the waitress can see her.

"Sure, do hun." She answers as she walks back over to the bar for a moment before coming back over handing medusa a menu.

"Anything else I can get started for you all?"

Taura puts in her own order of drinks, along with a few others. Once everyone who wanted to order at the moment finishes the waitress made her way back over to the bar letting one of the bartenders take over with our orders.

"Thank you, Calico! Next band on the agenda for tonight is Heaven's Gate followed by Eternal Voyage." Another male announces from on the stage.

"Who is that?" Taura asks as she looks towards the stage. Raiden lips twist up into a sly, know it all grin.

"That's my older brother Jacin. I'll call him over to come meet you all later. He was the one who set up everything for tonight, including finding the bands to play."

"Here are your drinks," the waitress says as she first sets down a blue crystal bowl with matching blue vials with glass and crystal tops. She then quickly unloads her other tray before we know it, she is gone.

"What are these?" Medusa asks as she grabs one of the vials.

Othello smiles. "These were created by accident, but we loved the results so we made it one of our specials. Each vial is filled with a different kind of drink. We usually make a huge batch for five different kinds and then fill up the bottles. Then we mix them up so even we won't know which is which. But aside from all of them having different tastes they also have fun side effects. One changes your hair color, another your eye color, voice, and so on. The effects only last for five minutes before you're back to your normal state."

"Okay we all need to try this out now." Taura squills before using her magic to place a vial in front of everyone.

"To a night full of memories, family and fun." Taura cheers before downing her drink.

"Cheers," the rest of us say before we empty our own vials. Medusa smiles as she looks at me.

"What happened to me?" I ask her.

"Well, I thought I liked you with blue flames, but the pink is more fitting." she says with a laugh.

"Do I have a different color of hair?" Taura asks but instead her normal higher pitched voice a deep timber sound comes out. Making all of us lose any control we had, which only grows more when Kyrell's laugh sounds like a duck quacking.

"Please give a huge welcome to Eternal Voyage." Jacin announces to the crowd.

" We need to get right up front now." Medusa shouts before she stands up on the seat and climbs right over Cooper to escape the booth with Taura closely following her. We all rush to follow them as they weave through the crowd to the front by the stage.

"Apparently you weren't the only one who drank a hair color changer." Cooper says as Medusa's snakes turn from green to purple and pink.

A couple of wankers' stepping into the space between us and the girls, a growl leaves my throat, as they lean down and whisper something into Medusa's ear. Her posture goes from loose and fun to stiff and straight. Stepping up behind the men we form a semi-circle around them.

"Excuse me." I say in what Octavius likes to call my authoritative voice.

"What do you want?" Douche Twinkie #1 says as he takes in my form before turning back to attempt to talk to Medusa.

Grabbing his arm, I twist him back towards me. "First off you can back away from our girls, I mean I can tell that you're stupid as fuck, but seriously. They're taken and you're making them uncomfortable." The asshat has the audacity to look back over at Medusa, before looking back at me and smirking.

"I don't see any bonding marks." He says with a smug smile. It makes me want to punch his teeth out with my fist and then reach through the opening and yank his soul out and disintegrate it. Denying him an afterlife at this point seems like a fitting punishment. Sadly, his friend is even more stupid than I thought he was.

"If you can prove to me, they are yours, we will leave them alone." Douche Twinkie #2 adds, just before two vines snatch him and his friend from our grasp.

"No need to prove anything." Medusa replies, her eyes glowing just like her snakes. I realize the vines came from her and her snakes are hissing fiercely, poised ready to bite. All of their heads focused on the scum buckets.

"Medusa, if you can tie them to the ceiling our Arachne

aerialists are up there, they will deal with them after the bar closes tonight." Othello tells her. With a slight nod the men are pulled up and disappear amongst the floral ceiling, hopefully to never be seen again.

"If they don't, we will make sure we do." Kyrell adds just before the lights dim. The only sounds are murmurs from the crowd and the soft steps from the stage as Octavius and his band mates get situated. Soon an all too familiar sound of an accordion starts to play, I've heard them practice enough times that I can count along with the beats in my sleep.

"Come with me now, Come with me now." Octavius sings out, just before the lights fill the stage. The Kraken keeps going, singing every word as more instruments join in on the party. Soon they are all performing their hearts out as they dance, play and sing.

"Why does this feel like I should be on a pirate ship?" I hear Medusa ask Taura as they both sway to the music. Stepping up behind her, I pull her closer to me till her sweet cheeks are pressed tightly against my front, swaying seductively with her, I lean down grazing my teeth against the side of her neck, then giving her earlobe a gentle nip.

"Because Octavius is a pirate." I growl against her ear. Before taking her delicate earlobe between my teeth and slowly pulling it through them before releasing it again. Only to smile as I watch her relax in my hold. We dance like that together till the song ends, and before I know it or can even protest, she is pulled out of my hold and Garen turns her to face him. I watch as their bodies move as one. The song Octavius is now singing seems to get more seductive in the beat. Yet our girl doesn't miss a beat, her moves are enticing, smooth, and alluring. Dipping his head down next to her ear.

"You look lovely tonight, Medusa." his voice sends shivers tingling up her spine.

"Thank you," Medusa replies. Garen winks and goes in to capture her lips, instead he meets air. I chuckle as I watch Ace slide in and take Medusa's lips for himself. Garen pouts but relents. Coming up for air, Ace winks at our bonded before turning his full attention back to Medusa.

"You all truly care about her." Raiden says, surprising me as he comes up next to me.

"We do." I answer honestly, as my true feelings for our snake goddess finally show their colors to me. I can no longer deny the pull to mate her and claim her as our center.

"Good because we wouldn't trust our center with any other men but you seven." he replies.

I nod my agreement. We would do everything in our power to keep Medusa happy, safe and give her anything she desires.

"Let's head back to the table, I need another drink," Taura shouts to Medusa just as Octavius's band finishes their last song.

"Can we try the Dirty Cupid?" Medusa asks her as they make their way back to our table.

CHAPTER 36

RAIDEN

For the first time in years my heart is pounding, and I feel nervous about the future that is being dangled right in front of me.

Medusa walked right into our lives. Unexpectedly perfect. Othello and I chatted all day when I got back from my run. We keep no secrets between us, funny enough that didn't start to happen until after I died.

Now everything has changed, not only did we find our center we found the rest of our bonded. Small holes in my soul now are patching themselves back together. Something that would have never happened if Othello hadn't been so stubborn. While I laid in bed weak, he put in the work to find a cure.

My heart broke at the time I thought it was a lost cause. Nightswish, a cruel sickness in our realm. An experience we agreed never to let anyone suffer from as we set up our coffee shop. Every brew has a special dosage to keep Nightswish at bay.

"Raiden are you okay?" Medusa's musical voice asks as she rests her hand on mine.

Smiling, "I'm fine, beautiful." I answer her.

"Are you sure you and Othello want to be with me? As you can see, I've got a lot of men in my life."

"We wouldn't want it any other way." I tell her honestly as I pull her hand up to mine, placing a gentle kiss against it.

"We won't be changing our minds anytime soon Medusa, plus Nero doesn't just like anyone." Othello adds as he tucks one of her snakes back from her cheek before laying his own mark on her.

"You sure about that?" Hades says while leaning over to hand medusa the last potion shot bottle.

"He met you all as well?" Othello asks.

"Yes," all the others say around the table.

"Good, that will make it easier when we have dinners together." I say just as another round of drinks arrive at the table.

"You going to introduce me to your new friends' brother?" Jacin asks while his eyes land hungrily on Taura.

"Everyone, this is Jacin, my brother. Jacin, meet Hades, Kyrell, Octavius, Everett, Taura, Medusa, Garen, Cooper and Ace."

"So Taura you with any of these fine men?" Jacin asks, making me wish a black hole would take him elsewhere. Not subtle bro, not subtle at all. Taura smirks, leaning her head on Octavius' shoulder.

"Who wants to know?" she asks flirtatiously.

"I do, along with my bonded." he answers her. Jacin is bold and honest almost to a fault.

"Well, when you put it that way, no I'm not with any of these guys. They all belong to her." Taura says as she hitches her thumb over towards Medusa.

"They don't belong to me." Medusa replies.

"They do too. Now Jacin, let's go meet these bonded of

yours. Medusa behave yourself while I'm gone." Taura tells Medusa as she climbs over the back of the booth.

"Nice meeting you all." Jacin says quickly before rushing over to Taura. He holds out the crook of his arm for her to take. He then guides her a few tables over, to where he and his bonded have been occupying.

"Would you guys like to come over to our house for dinner tomorrow?" Hades asks us.

"We'd love to, plus it means we get to spend more time getting to know you all and Medusa." Othello replies as I nod my agreement.

"Don't forget to bring Nero." Medusa instructs us.

"We never would forget him." I promise, even though I'm sure the beasty creature will already be cuddling up with Medusa hours before we arrive.

CHAPTER 37
ATTICUS

Leaning against the wall I slide down to the ground in my hut on Oceania Island. Tomorrow I will check out the other side of the island. With the simple means of their buildings and homes I had no idea there was so much more to this place I was wrong. After they showed me the way back to their home, I was surprised to see they have a whole functioning city one that has rivers of water passing through every street. With pathways and bridges for those who don't want to or can't swim.

King Kalon and Queen Sitara were incredibly helpful after they decided I was no longer a threat. They took me back to their incredible village Aequoreal. A mixture of supernaturals and Mermaids. Smiling as they watch their children run around playing with each other never judging each other's differences. King Kalon explained how they set up floating docks for those who are too far out to sea and unable to make it to shore by swimming. A lot of those who arrive are supernaturals searching for a better life, or are running for their lives. Occasionally some wash up that were sailing and got hit by a bad storm.

"Feel free to check out the resort as well. Not all arrivals show up here," Queen Sitara added as we walked through the recent arrivals to the island this morning.

None of which were Medusa.

After a long day of searching, they invited me back to their home. Fed me dinner and even allowed me to stay in one of their many guest huts.

Once I do find Medusa, I will have to introduce her to my new friends here. The mermaids and their mates. I think she'd love. Plus, all the exotic plants and animals that roam here. She'd never want to leave.

Looking over the map one last time before rolling it up and placing it back in my bag.

Laying down on the bed staring up at the skylight. I can see the stars above. "Don't worry Medusa, I'll find you," I say into the night before letting my eyes close.

CHAPTER 38

GAREN

"Note to self-make sure the next time I get cursed they give me super ninja powers because training sucks Lamassu ball." Medusa groans after Kyrell knocks her on her back again.

Holding out my hand to help her back up, "You're doing great Medusa, just ten more times with that sequence and we will go eat breakfast," I tell her, hoping to entice her into keep going. I know soon she will see how right I have been when I told her I could turn her into a bad ass snake goddess.

"Fine one last sequence then someone better feed me, these snakes and I are starting to feel a little bitey."

Circling her and Kyrell as they start again. My eyes following every step, punch, and movement, making sure Medusa hits all the points exactly as I showed her.

"There better be a pot of coffee with a straw in it waiting for me after this," she replies while blocking another of Kyrell's hits. A devious idea comes to me, I let Kyrell know my plan as move in closer to until I'm so close she can feel my breath fanning the back of her neck.

"Don't worry my Musa, Ace promised you all the coffee your heart could want. He won't disappoint you." My words whisper across her skin, causing her to shiver. She turns quickly to face me. Desire flames to life, dancing in her eyes. Medusa leans into me, closing her eyes. I smile before I wrap my hand behind her neck, pulling Musa in closer, pressing my lips to hers. Slowly I start to walk until I have her back against the cool brick. Grasping her hands, pinning them against the wall above her head.

It isn't until she hears the click of the cuffs that she realizes what has happened, "Never let yourself get distracted, it will give your opponent the chance they need to defeat you." I advise her while looking into her eyes.

"Got it, so use distractions on them," She replies.

"Exactly." I answer, stepping back.

"Are you going to let me go?" Medusa asks while raising a brow.

"In a moment," I answer my eyes, taking a mental picture to help me through the days till I get the chance to explore her body. With one last look, I reluctantly keep my word moving slowly. I dig in my pocket pulling out a small gold key. I insert it taking my time as I unlock the cuffs one at a time, freeing her.

"Grab your sword, let's try this again," I instruct her while Kyrell steps off to the side of the room.

The moment she pulls the sword off the wall I go in for the attack, she twirls around blocking my move. Dancing back and forth as our swords clash against each other. Medusa makes many attempts to hit me with tricks to win, but what she doesn't realize she gives many telling signs of her next move. With my eyes watching every movement that my mate makes. Soon I have Medusa on her back with my sword pointed down at her throat. Her snakes seem to be watching me, while she calculates a way out of this.

"Do you cave, Medusa?" I ask. Her eyes narrow, slightly shifting from her beautiful amethyst eyes to a more of a deeper purple as her pupils become slender, like snakes.

"I'm just getting started," she replies, with fire and determination.

It's so adorable it's making the side of my mouth quirk upward.

"Then show me what you have, sweetheart."

I should have known from that look she'd be full of surprises. The next thing I know I'm on the ground, tied down by strong vines that shoot out of the ground twining themselves around my legs and torso while more pull my hands above my head. Medusa stands gracefully, picking up my sword, twirling it a few times before pointing it at me. No longer is she the scared woman from that first night she arrived in our home. Standing before me, now is a Goddess of ancient power. How the other gods ever thought her to be weak I'll never know.

"I believe that means I win," Medusa says as her eyes return to normal, snapping her fingers, the vines disappear back into the dirt floor of our training room.

"It does. Why do I get the feeling you have been playing games with me?" I ask with a laugh. She shrugs her shoulders elegantly; a secretive smile graces her luscious lips. Taunting me. I know that whatever she's about to say will be a revealing truth. One she rarely acknowledges.

"I am the Goddess of creatures and nature. I was never thought to be strong, but the thing is I have control over the two fiercest things that every realm has. I could bring cities to dust if I willed it all with the snap of my finger, or order creatures of all kinds to rain down on and attack my enemies. All this power stored in my being and yet I never used them in this manner unless I had no other choice." She replies.

"That's because you are a true Goddess, one who doesn't abuse her powers. And I'm so lucky that I get to call you mine." I reply, my words seeming to have a strange effect on her.

I wasn't wasting another minute, Medusa deserved to know my feelings, the way just the sight of her has my fingers yearning to touch her, while my mouth craves to taste her, my soul calling out for hers. I crave her like I have no other female, nor do I wish to. She has curves more dangerous than any mountain road and I wanted nothing more hen to trace them while she begged for her release. Tied to my bed while trusting me fully, a daydream I have had daily. My creature wanted us to take her, but we would wait until she gave us the command. Sucking in a deep breath of her sweet scent filling my lungs as it consumes all of my senses.

"I take it you're not one to wait around to announce when something is yours?" she challenges, as her eyes for a moment dip to my lips before returning to meet my stare.

"Not anymore. I'm tired of holding back on how you make me feel. I crave you like you are the sweetest chocolate. Don't worry my goddess, I will wait for you to admit you are ready for more than my sweet kisses." I whisper against her lips.

Stepping away from her, "Tell me Medusa, what is it that you want?" I ask as I take the sword from her walking back over to the wall of weapons and placing it back on its stand.

She is next to me in an instant, surprising me with how silent she can be. "I want to experience everything this world has to offer me." Medusa announces as her eyes trail up my body.

"And you will," I promise Medusa as I take her hands in mine, before pulling her into my arms. "We will give you the world," I whisper.

"Why?" she asks, her large doe eyes burning into mine.

"Because you, my love, are our center. You're our everything." I tell her before swooping in and pressing my lips against her soft sensual lips.

My Kipin begins purring as Medusa encourages the kiss, adding to the fire that seems to be consuming our being. Till our souls are caressing each other. I want nothing more than to show her in every way what she does to me, how she makes me feel. Share with her all the fantasies I've been dreaming of since I first laid my eyes on her.

CHAPTER 39
MEDUSA

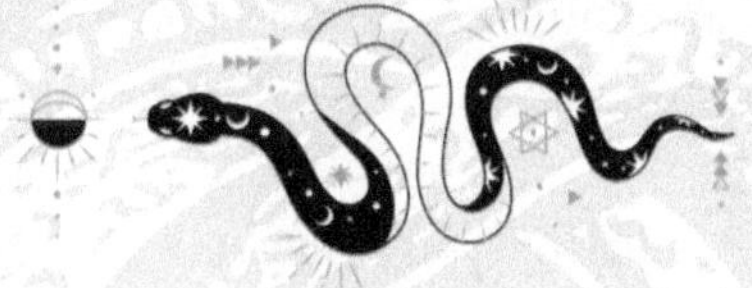

Their center? Me? I'm not even sure how to be a center? Are there certain expectations they will have for me? Could I keep them all happy? Would I even have enough hours in the day to spend time with them? Would I have to give up things I love doing or would it all be like it is now?

"How does the whole center and bonded thing work?" I blurt out. My timing must be off because all the guys start choking on something or almost spit out their drinks.

"What would you like to know?" Taura asks as she leans to the side in her chair.

"Just how it all works, and I'm not just talking about the sex part." Closing my eyes, I take a deep breath as I get my thoughts together, "What I'm trying to ask if it will be like we are now or are there certain expectations. Like cooking or cleaning? Be warned I'm a horrible cook. Or Am I expected to spend time with you all, all the time. Or will I still have my freedom to run off and get a coffee with Taura, go for a walk in the woods. I just want to know what it all means." I finish slumping in my chair feeling a little better after getting all my inner ramblings out.

"First off here is your coffee Medusa." Ace says, handing me a big mug of my life juice. "Secondly, we just want you to be you. We don't expect much from you because we want you just the way you are, we want every flaw and imperfection, every weakness just as much as we want the rest."

"We want you for you Medusa. Not as a slave or a possession and not for any reason other than the fact that you complete us and bring so much light into our lives." Hades replies, shocking me with his words that do weird things to my heart.

Someone pinch me. Looking around the table at each of my guys for the first time I truly notice how they all are looking at me like I'm the best thing since coffee.

"Medusa you have nothing to worry about, we would never push you to do anything you don't want to. We also would never ask you to clean without helping. This place is ginormous, Taura has already spelled 80% of the house to clean itself. All we ask as you give us a chance to prove our worth to you." Hades adds as he stands out of his chair and walks around till, he is standing next to me before he drops down till, he is kneeling and closer to my eye level.

Damn it he is still taller than me. I sit up a little taller to try and get on eye level. A sigh escapes my lips, before I give him my full attention.

"Medusa when you first arrived on our island, I thought you were a trick. I was terrified you had come here to bring nothing but ill intentions."

"Where are you going with this?" I ask not truly getting what he is trying to say.

"Just listen, I promise it comes together at the end." Hades whispers as he boops my nose.

"Fine."

"Now where was I?"

"Ill intentions." Taura reminds him.

"Ah yes, Medusa aside from our rocky start, mostly because of me. I want to ask you if you will be our center?" Looking around the room at all the men and I notice they are smiling. "Yes. I'll be your center." I answer just before Hades pulls me out of the chair and into his arms, moments before his lips slam down on mine. Stealing my breath as I melt like butter against him. Pulling away, "wait what about Othello and Raiden?"

"We won't do the bonding ceremony without them." Hades promises before his lips conquered mine once more, just before one of the other guys steals me from his hold. I smile when I come face to face with Garen.

"Now I can have you anytime I want." He whispers in my ear, the deep timber in his voice makes me shiver with excitement of what is to come. I'm about to reply but before I can, I'm pulled into another pair of arms, silver globes of moonlight stare down into my soul.

"I know you'd be ours from the moment I saw you." Everetts says while lowering till his lips brushed against mine sweeping me into an earth-shattering kiss. My hands ran up his chest until they were entwined in his hair, keeping him secured to me.

"She has others here who like a chance to devour her." Octavius says making Everett break our kiss, I look up chuckling as I can see him giving the kraken the stink eye. While he was distracted by Octavius, Ace used his shadow magic to pull me from Everett's hold.

"Are you sure you can handle all this, all the time love?"

Ace asks me, his words making the others pause. Smiling, I look around the room, minus the few of my men missing this moment. I wouldn't want to be anywhere else but with them. I see now this is why I never felt at home in Karpathos.

"I'm where I want to be."

CHAPTER 40
HADES

"Medusa," I yell through the house, as I head towards the library. She is just as bad as the rest of us, it's become one of her favorite places to hide out. Not that I blame her with four levels each one filled with books about everything it's a secret treasure to behold. I smile as I come to a stop in the doorway. Medusa is laying by the fireplace lost in a book while her head rests on Nero. It's a scene I'll have to paint later in my private art studio.

"Medusa," I say gently as I walk into the room. Looking over the book, she smiles while sitting up and stretching.

"A good book?" I ask while I join her on the floor.

"Incredibly good," she replies, "So what do I owe the pleasure of seeing you here?"

"I was just wondering if you would like to go for a walk?" I ask her. Not mentioning my other plan for this walk, which is a surprise, but I need her with me so I can find the perfect place to build it.

"I'd love to," she replies.

Standing up before offering her my hand, Medusa

doesn't disappoint me as she gives me one of her sweet smiles while taking my hand in hers, I pull her up. I'm half tempted to devour her lips. But I remined myself there will be plenty of time for that, once we get to my favorite hidden gems we have here on our property. It's a place that I'm sure will quickly become Medusa's new favorite spot. The moment we are outside I lead her down a side path that leads to a hidden waterfall with a pond.

"Where are we going Hades?" she asks me.

"If I told you, then how am I to surprise you?" I reply teasingly.

"I can pretend to be surprised." I look back over at her, Medusa's tongue peeks out sweeping in a slow crest over her pouty lips teasing me. Desire races through my veins, I wanted nothing more than to indulge in her pretty flesh.

"Quit testing my patience, woman." I mutter loud enough for her to hear. "But no, I will not succumb to your seductive teasing, nor will I cave and ruin the surprise."

She pouts playfully at me, her luscious lips not playing fair. I was then swept in another wave of lust as her musical laugh filled the space between us. Too much space if you asked me. Stepping out of the forest trail Medusa gasps as she freezes in place, before us was the hidden waterfall, the large clear pond that is surrounded by wildflowers and soft grass. With tall trees skirting around the place keeping, it tucked away from prying eyes.

"This is beautiful." Medusa says in awe, while letting go of my hand as she steps closer to the water as if she can't help but be drawn in by its beauty.

"It's just like the pond I had by my place in the Evercrest Forest.

"I'd say I'm surprised, but the Evercrest Forest has

magic all on its own." I reply as I capture her hand once more.

"It feels like home here," She replies to me.

"This is one of my favorite places to hide out and think." I tell her as I sit down by the edge of the pond. Pulling her down with me settling her between my legs, her back resting against my chest. Medusa turns her attention to the water, her fingertips caress my knee as she looks out and takes in the view. Kissing the top of her head while breathing in her delectable scent, I feel my soul settle at how perfect this feels, how right.

"We've waited for what feels like a lifetime for you," I tell her. "I'd destroy worlds for you, all you have to do is ask." I whisper against her neck, before pressing a kiss to the tender flesh there.

Tilting her head back to look up at me, I lean forward pressing my lips to hers softly before my kiss turns into a passion of hell fire. I broke apart long enough to spin her in my lap. I claimed her lips, showing her everything I felt, everything that I was, it was possessive, a way for me to mark her as mine. I lift her up, before setting her back down so that she now straddles me.

Medusa doesn't stop there, and she pushes against me until I find myself lying on the grass. Her thighs straddling my waist a moan slipping out of her perfect lips causing my already hard dick to press against my waist band, I'm so fucking hard it's almost painful.

Grabbing her hips, I thrust up pulling her center against me. Grinding my hard-on into her as I nip and suck on her lips. Medusa releases another moan. Fuck those sounds is like a siren call. Flipping our positions so she lays on her back, under me on the soft grass.

"If we keep going, I make no promises I'll stop till you

are screaming my name." I tell her, I don't want her to feel like she isn't in charge here.

"I want this Hades, I want you." She tells me. Nodding, I grab her top ripping it down the center, tearing through the lacey bra she has on as well.

"I hope you weren't too attached to your shirt." I say as I take in her chest. Two perky globes begging me to taste them as her nipples acting as anchors.

"Not at all Octavius bought me fifteen of the same one." She replies, a moan slipping out as I suck one of her nipples. Swirling my tongue around before I draw more into my mouth.

The scent of her arousal fills the air, I switch over to her other nipple. My thumb and forefinger tease the taut bud of her exposed nipple, small whimpers leave her lips. Grinning, I switch back taking the nipple deep between my tongue and teeth before flicking my tongue over it to soothe the pain before I repeat. When she is nothing but a quivering mess, I kiss my way down the slope of her breast, trailing my lips and tongue down her torso nipping her stomach before I get to the edge of her pants.

"These will need to go as well." I tell her before I rip her bottoms like I did to her top. A sharp gasp escapes her lips the moment she is completely bare to me. Giving her body a bold sweeping gaze, every inch of this woman is calling for me to touch it, to mark it and taste it. Her pussy is glistening in the sun as her sweet nectar leaks from her lips. While watching her I let my fingers run across her seam. I smile as she shivers from the pleasure.

"Hades please." she begs in a sexy whimper that almost breaks me.

Swirling my fingers, I spread her lips apart before sinking one into her, her hips moved along with my finger moving faster. Pumping it in and out before adding another and another until she writhed against my hand, lost in her own pleasure. Pulling my fingers free, causing a slight hiss to leave her lips.

Chuckling I bend down licking up her seam before I dive right in drinking in her taste. How any woman could taste as sweet as honey I'll never know but Medusa does. Parting her lips, I plunge my tongue into her feeling how tight she is as I lather up her sweet nectar. Her fingers lace into my hair as she starts riding my face. I suck and slurp her pussy up as she sets the pace, I add a finger into the mix.

"Hades," her plea makes my name sound like a prayer that only I can answer.

"Yes, my love?" I reply before dipping my tongue back into her.

"I'm... I'm... " She doesn't finish. The ability to speak has apparently deserted her, as I feel her walls tighten clenching and drenching my fingers as her orgasm takes over. Her sweet nectar is coating my tongue and hand as my stunningly beautiful seductress screams out my name with her release. I pull back, watching my goddess in her pure bliss.

Standing I whip off my shirt. Medusa's up on her knees before me looking like my favorite wet dream. Her trembling hands unbutton my jeans, before her fingers tug my zipper down. Her eyes devour my length, looking too eager to tame the serpent my pants were trying to hide. My hardness sprang mercifully free from its prison.

She stared hungrily at my shaft as she wraps one slender hand around my erection and begins to move it back and forth. She pulls the hard flesh faster before surprising me and taking it into her sinfully, wicked mouth. Medusa's mouth worships my altar, taking me in with devout desire.

"Lay down Medusa," I command her as I pull my cock free from her mouth. Obeying me she lays down in the grass spreading her thighs wide to receive me. "You sure you want this? There is no going back after we do this. I'll be yours even when we move onto the afterlife." I tell her pressing the tip of my erection against her slick folds.

"I want it all Hades. I want you and the others." She tells me. I bend down kissing her, while pushing myself into the heated core of her body. Before pulling back almost all the way, then plunging back into her depths. A sweet moan leaves her lips, as she arches her hips, Medusa meets me thrust for thrust.

Without warning I pull out of her, flipping her with ease before thrusting back into her from behind, clasping her hips in a tight grip, pulling them hard against me. Fucking her hard and fast, I feel my balls starting to tighten. I pull her up so her back is flat against my chest. I watch as her fingers work her clit while I'm pounding into her. I'm bespelled, watching as Medusa becomes a hellcat, as I fuck her, all wet, and wild with need.

Making a last-minute decision using my nail I slice my wrist and then I slice the corner of her neck. Pressing my wrist against her lips Medusa drinks in my blood as her second orgasm shatters my world. I drink in her blood as my come coats the inside of her pussy, which clenches around me as it milks me of every last drop.

Eventually I pull out of her, laying back onto the cool grass pulling my mate onto me, cradling her chest against mine. Running my fingers through her hair, I smile as I feel our bond seal itself. There is now no doubt left in my mind that this perfect snake goddess is mine. Lifting her head up, she smiles lovingly down at me.

"Ready to go again?" She asks, as her hand snakes down to my cock that is already growing hard.

"This time you get to be on top." I tell her as I grab her by the waist and spear her with my cock her damp entrance swallowing me in one swift plunge. Straddling me her hips began grinding before she lifted her hips up and spearing herself back down on my cock moaning as it filled her back up. She did it again and again, fucking me like she owned me as she sought out her climax as she rode me hard and fast.

It was taking everything in me to hold on just a little longer, I grunted grasping her hips I began pounding hard into her until I cried out in pure pleasure at the same moment, she screams my name. My hot seed coating her walls, while her body spasmed around me until she was finally done and laid down on my chest. My hands tracing the contours of her body in soft caresses while I kiss the top of her head.

Standing up with her in my hold I walk us over to the pond and step right in. Smiling, she locks her legs around my waist before leaning back, allowing herself to just float. Chuckling, I pull her back into me.

"I don't think the snakes liked that much." I tell her as I nuzzle into her neck.

"They can deal with it, they got enough of a show today." she tells me, causing a surprise of barking laughter to flow out from me.

"I love you, Hades." she tells me before pressing her lips to mine. Pulling apart, my chest swells with all the love I feel for her.

"I love you too, Medusa."

CHAPTER 41

HADES

Swimming had worn Medusa out so much she fell asleep while we floated around in the cool water. I had to climb out of the pond with her in my arms. Once back on dry land, I found a spot in the sun to lay down so we can dry out before heading back to the house.

Medusa murmurs nonsense as she cuddles more securely into my side, her snakes' fan out so they can all get warmed by the sun. The moment is absolutely perfect! For the first time in centuries, I wish my powers included the power of time. I'd give anything for the ability to freeze this perfect moment.

"Lulu?" Medusa says as she shoots up, almost knocking heads with me. Her head swivels back and forth as she looks around before her gaze becomes fixated at the far end of the field across from us. That's when I sit up in shock, Aequilla's? I haven't seen these splendid creatures that used to roam our island in centuries. Not since my brother stole them from their home. Medusa in an instant, is up and running right up to a light pink one with magenta fur, "Oh Lulu how did you get here?" She asks the creature out loud.

While she continues to look over Lulu and the other Aequilla's it's then I realized that Medusa would need a bigger sanctuary than I originally thought. Caring for these animals and any other creatures that found her, or any she found that needed help was going to take a heck of a lot of room. It would be worth it though just to see the smile that graces her beautiful face. Getting dressed while I watch Medusa, thinking over my original idea compared to seeing her in action, I formulate a plan of what we will need to build for her.

"Hades, come meet Lulu and the other Aequilla's." Medusa calls me over. How could I resist her request? Walking over to her side I slip my shirt over her head just as Medusa begins to tell me each Anguilla's names. After a few hours of hanging out with the Aequilla's Medusa's stomach rumbles and the air grows colder.

"Let's get you home and fed, my little goddess." I whisper to her.

"Okay just let me say goodbye to Lulu." she tells me as she walks over to the Aequilla who seems to be the leader of this herd. Once Medusa has said her goodbye to her creature friend, we make the trek through the forest.

Of course, that was not to be the end of our unpredictable day. On our way back Medusa is suddenly grabbed by large brittlely vines. I run quickly after her knowing exactly what has just taken her. Only to stop in surprise as I find my tiny goddess sitting there talking with a Snapdragon Hydnora, also known as Dragon Snap. This particular one is as large as Everett, and I combined. It reminds of a Piranha Plant but larger with teeth like a dragon and the petals that cover it are like dragon scales. Normally Cooper and Taura use their magic to relocate them away from our home, but the damn things can uproot and move to a new spot or even chase you.

"Hades, come say hi to Lizzy." Medusa says waving me over before she continues talking to Lizzy. My tiny goddess seems to name plants as well as animals. She is absolutely adorable, and seemingly so unaware of the danger she is in. I have a feeling this is going to be how she introduces us all to all the creatures or strange creature plants she meets.

Cautiously I walk over to them, still trying to really think over and sort out in my mind what was going on. I knew Medusa had nature gifts, but this is just wild. Everything in me is screaming to scoop up my mate and run for safety.

"She won't bite, honestly most Dragon Snaps are just very mischievous, but they only eat bugs and small prey." Medusa explains to me.

"Really?" I ask as I feel a little more comfortable getting closer.

"It's okay Lizzy, you won't have to hide out in the forest ever again." Medusa tells the plant creature. I lay a gentle hand on Lizzy, the scale-like shell is as soft as rose petals, smiling over I look over at Medusa, my heart ever so slightly more ensnared with my tiny goddess than I was before.

"No, she won't."

After taking Lizzy over to the waterfall and finding her a perfect spot to rest, Medusa and I finally make the trek back to the house. With one look at Medusa's new clothing, they all instantly know exactly what we have been up to in the forest.

"You really had wild forest sex without me." Octavius whines, making Medusa chuckle as the guys berate me.

"It wasn't planned." I admit to them. Garen stands up giving Medusa his arm.

"Come on beautiful, let's get a bath started for you."

"That sounds nice." Medusa admits as she takes his offered arm. "Go easy on Hades, it really wasn't planned." she says while heading up to her suite. Another situation we will have to deal with, as we move her down to our floor.

While they're gone the others give me a hard time. I explain to them about Lizzy in case they run into the Dragon Snap around the house and try to make her hide away again. I'm pretty sure that thing followed us home, even after Medusa found Lizzy the perfect spot by the waterfall.

After five minutes Garen comes back down smiling like the cat that got the cream. Shaking my head, I realize I can't be too mad at him. But I will be the one with the last laugh when Lizzy surprises him. It's not my fault he skipped out.

"I want to build her a cabin by the pond to tend to her creatures." I tell the others before diving into exactly what I witnessed today with the Aequilla's. With all of us agreeing to help build it, I make a quick call using our mirror to let Othello and Raiden in on our plan. Once I finish talking with them, we all make our way to the kitchen to start on dinner. Chicken parmesan. While I dice up tomatoes for our salad, I think over everything Medusa's cabin would need.

"We're going to have to tell Medusa about the cabin." I blurt out.

"I hate to admit it, but I was wondering how we were going to figure out everything that she would need for it." Kyrell adds as he seasons up the chicken.

"Exactly, but once I have a detailed, itemized list, she isn't allowed to see it until it's done." I tell them.

"Who isn't allowed to see what?" I hear Medusa ask as

she enters the room dressed in one of Garen's shirts. Even in the oversized clothing the sight of her leaves me breathless. Love fills my heart as I look her over.

"We want to build you a cabin so you can take better care of the animals that come to you." I excitedly tell her. Her smile at my comment doesn't just light up her face but the whole room.

"Really?" she asks in wonderment, the happy surprise filtering through her stunning features.

"Really," I answer as I give her a wink.

"Damn maybe I should have fucked you sooner." she tells me as she walks by stealing a carrot while giving me a cheeky grin.

"Naughty, naughty, Medusa," Octavius tsks at her, "You know what naughty girls get?"

"No, what do naughty girls get?" she asks Octavius her big purple eyes dilated as notes of her sweet nectar fill the air. Placing two fingers up her chin he lifts her gaze up to his.

"They get punished." he purrs out before scooping her up and tossing her over his shoulder giving us all a sweet show. "No underwear love. You are a naughty girl."

"Octavius put me down." Medusas says just before he brings a hand down onto her ass cheeks. Causing her breath to hitch. Octavius moves with quick but supple grace, and he carries Medusa off, intending to carry her to our room. The rest of us following closely behind them.

"Where are you all going? And why isn't food done?" Taura asks from the kitchen.

"Fun spoiler," Cooper grumbles as he pulls Medusa free from Octavius's hold and sets her back down. The look on her face says she isn't happy we are choosing food over the fun we were about to have. The sexual frustration now radiating through every member of our bond echoes it.

"Such an appetite you have." I whisper before nipping her ear as I walk by her.

CHAPTER 42
HADES

Early the next morning Medusa and I walk over to the pond to confirm that the spot I picked was indeed where she would want to build her little cabin.

"What about here?" I ask her, my heart anxiously awaiting her approval of the spot I have picked.

"That's a good spot, oh what about right over there?" she asks as she walks towards a spot that has two giant oak trees. It is close to the pond. "The front could face this way with maybe some large windows to see the pond." she suggests just as I come up behind her pulling her into my arms.

"It's perfect." I tell her before gently nibbling on her ear.

"Stop that you tease." she tells me as she wiggles out of my hold to face me. Medusa is smiling with a mischievous gleam in her eye before she takes off running across the field. Musical laughter trails after her as she heads into the trees nearby.

"Now who is being a tease," I shout as I move to make chase. Medusa isn't being quiet as she runs. I can hear her sweet giggles as she runs through the forest.

A particularly friendly vine grabs my wrists as Medusa skips right by me before disappearing in the foliage again. My center is in her element, it brings so much joy to my heart to see her so free to be herself. Finally, I free myself and follow after her. Only to come to pause when I see her growing and dancing across giant mushrooms. Her movements are flawless as if she is just floating in the air. I step onto the first one and dance my way over to her. Finally reaching her I grab her hand in mine, pulling her into me as we start to waltz across more mushrooms that continue to grow. Eventually Medusa and I make our way back down to the ground ending our dance.

"Let's get back so I can let the others know where we are building the cabin." I tell her while intertwining our fingers together. Her hand fits so perfectly in mine it feels like this is the way it was always meant to be. "So, what was your old cabin in the Evercrest Forest like?" I ask, wanting to make sure we give her everything she will need.

"My old place wasn't too big, but it did have a nice living room with a fireplace, where owners or friends could hang out. My kitchen was large with a long island where I could prepare the food for the many animals that came into my care. I even had a bath ..." stopping in place her face frozen as her eyes searching for something. I look around for any threats.

"Medusa is everything okay?" I ask, as I mentally get ready to call for the others.

"A creature is hurt." She says, before turning on her heel, heading off into the trees. I follow her, making sure she doesn't get hurt in the process of trying to help an injured animal. We don't get too far in before she rounds a tree there curled up in a ball is the strangest creature I've ever seen covered in blood.

"It's a mole," she explains, "he's lost lots of blood. We need to get him to the animal sanctuary." She says as she carefully strips off of her sweater, wrapping it around the mole before picking him up gently and rushing back to the house.

"Cooper get a portal ready. We have a hurt creature and Medusa needs to get it to the animal sanctuary now." I say through the bond with my other mates.

"Everything will be okay, Medusa," I tell her as I run beside her, guiding her towards where Cooper and the others are waiting for us.

The moment we are close enough we rush forward through the portal, all of us going, knowing on some end she will need us all for this moment.

I just hope it has a happy ending for the creature.

CHAPTER 43
MEDUSA

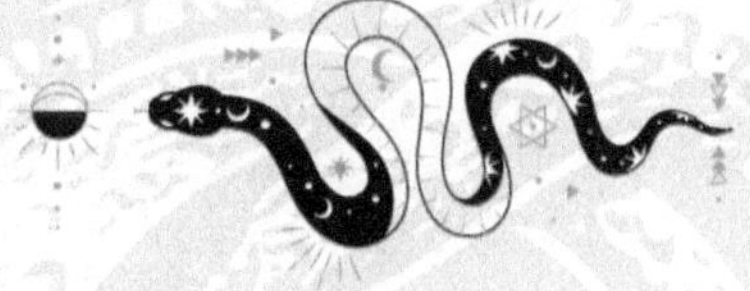

The moment I step out of the portal I am running. I can feel him fading with every second that ticks by. Rushing through the doors, Hades and Cooper run on either side of me, the others are only mere steps behind us.

"Can I help you?" the woman at the counter asks.

"I have a creature who has lost a lot of blood. I can feel him fading as we speak." I quickly explained, not even bothering to be polite.

"Let me take him, I promise we will help him." She says. The second I set the mole in her arms, she disappears through a door that was behind her desk. I turn to face the guys, Cooper pulls me into him.

"Hugs help." He says as the tears I've been holding back now run freely down my face. My mind wandering back as I wonder if there was anything I could have done. Without having my cabin full of my tools and herbs I doubt that there was anything else I could have done. Now I had to trust others to help the mole.

"What if we didn't get him here in time?" I mumble into Coopers chest.

"Then it was meant to be. But at least he knew he had someone who cared enough to bring him here to get help." Ace tells me.

I turn my head to look at him, "Thank you." I mouth, while clinging onto Cooper.

"You know, maybe we should take her to see the creatures in the field." I hear Hades say.

"Can we?" I ask, intrigued to see more of this place.

"Yes, we can," he says as he starts walking.

Cooper lets me pull away only to snag my hand as we follow Hades through some giant oak doors with Lilly's etched into them. The moment we step outside, I'm shocked what lays beyond the doors. A small forest of red oak trees stands tall, their leaves making perfect domes, a lazy creek flows through the middle, leading to a small pond in the distance. Creatures of all kinds walk around eating the grass, chasing each other, or resting and watching the other animals. Under the largest tree, I see the rare sight of a Zark Wolf. Her fur is a pearlescence white, her belly round.

"Hello, Goddess of Creatures," she says to me.

I bow my head, "Hello, Guardian of Gods and Goddesses." I reply before letting go of Coopers hand and walking over to her slowly.

Once I reach her, I sit down next to her, "May I?" I ask her. She nods her head, giving me her permission. I then gently place my hand on her stomach and smile when I feel her pups move, and then I feel the contraction that slams into her.

"They're coming."

"If you allow me to, I can help you."

"I trust you and your mates, Goddess." She answers, I feel the genuineness in her words.

"It will be an honor," I tell her softly before turning my head towards the guys, "Can you guys run back into the hospital? I need towels and some warm water, and anything they have for birthing Zark Wolfs." I tell them before turning my attention back to the guardian.

"Do you want to shift or stay in your wolf form?" I ask her.

"I heal faster in wolf form. And please, call me Vera," she tells me.

"Alright, Vera," I say with a smile. She doesn't reply as her contractions grow. Throwing her head back; she howls, her tail lifting slightly just as a small black puppy makes its way out.

"Give the pup to me." I hear Ace say as he is waiting with a towel. I pick up the little one, handing it over to Ace while he cleans it up from the blood and after birth, before gently placing it in a large soft animal bed that Hades and Garen have set up next to Vera's head.

"Another is coming." She says to me, I'm ready this time with a pile of soft warm towels to wrap the pups up in as they are born, one after another. By the time Vera is done, we have seven healthy pups, two females and five males.

I smile, watching Vera as she cleans her pups up before shifting. Vera is just as beautiful as she is in her Wolf form, long pearlescent hair flows behind her. Her skin is pale as the moon. Silver eyes and red lips. She is stunning, if I didn't just see her shift, I'd have mistaken her as the winter fae queen. Hades hands me a robe for her before turning to face the other way. I look back to see the guys have their backs to us, giving Vera the privacy, she deserves. Standing, I walk over behind her helping her into the robe.

"Thank you, Goddess." Vera says, tying the sash of the robe securely around her waist.

"Please call me Medusa. As you can see, I'm no longer just a goddess."

"Well then, thank you Medusa, and mates of Medusa. You all are so kind as to help me."

"It was nothing, we just happened to be here at the right time."

"That you were. And for that I owe you a debt," she tells me.

"How about just a friendship," I reply, not feeling that helping her, well mostly sitting with her as she gave birth, wasn't truly debt worthy.

Her lips curved up into a soft smile, "You are not like the other gods and goddesses I've met before. But I will admit I love the sound of having you as my friend."

"We have a guest suite if you would like to stay there." I hear Hades say, as I feel the guys step up behind me.

"It seems the fates are smiling down on me today," Vera says just as I hear a clucky growl. I turn quickly to see my familiar.

"Loki?" I say, standing, tripping a little as I rush over to the tortoise making his way to me fairly quickly. I didn't know he could move that fast. How is he moving that fast? Honestly, I don't care, Loki is here.

"Medusa, do you know this creature?" I hear Kyrell ask.

"Yes, he is my familiar," I answer, kneeling on the ground, wrapping my arms awkwardly around his neck. I smile. "How the hell did you get here Loki?" I ask.

"He was sent to us from Karpathos, he and his mate arrived with this letter." says a woman that has leaves for hair. "It explained his uniqueness as a familiar, I'll admit this is a first in all my years of seeing a tortoise as a familiar for a goddess," she adds with a smile.

"You should have seen my face when he first appeared to me," I reply as I think back to the day, I met Loki. "I had decided to make a picnic for me and my best friend. I had a lot of fruits and veggies set up for me and Atticus. While waiting for him to arrive, I set up our plates. I had turned my head as I heard the sound of wings in the air. A munching sound had me jump off the ground and my own wings popping out and wrapping me up in their safe embrace." I say chuckling at the memory, "Then something rammed into me making all sorts of noises. It was this fierce guy trying to save me from my own wings." I say before kissing Loki's head gently as he croons back at me.

CHAPTER 44
ATTICUS

Hiding under some palm trees watching the ocean. Doubt filling my mind with thoughts that I will never find Medusa ever again. I've searched all through the resort on this part of the island. And the only thing I've found is that some mermaids are more forward than I would have thought. One even licked me while saying 'He is mine now, bitches.'

After escaping the pool of mermaids, that I had wandered into. I found my way here, just as the coast had cleared and head back to my hut a warlock walks by with an elemental mage who seems fond of tossing a fire ball up in the air.

"I'm telling you the truth, Hades has finally found himself a woman. She is even a gorgon. A pretty one at that."

"I didn't know any gorgons were living in Zakynthos." His friend replied as they headed towards a hut at the end of the path. I follow as close as I can behind them, in hopes of gathering more information.

"Are you going to ask what you need to ask, young god,

or are you going to keep hiding in the shadows?" The warlock asks me.

Being caught I had no choice but to step out to stand before the two of them. "I need to go to Zakynthos," I say.

"And why would a god such as yourself want to go to a monster island?"

"My mate may be there,"

The warlock turns to face me. "Well then, I guess we can take you there. For a price."

"What do you want?" I ask.

"Just a favor."

"As long as it doesn't involve killing, giving you my powers, or my first-born child."

The warlock laughs, "No nothing like that. But I do get to call on the favor whenever I choose. Do we have a deal, God?" he asks, holding out his hand. I glare at it, wondering if I could just enter without his help. But I was running out of options and worse case, if Medusa wasn't on the island, I'd never see this man again. I place my hand in his.

"Deal," I say as a burning sensation sears into the palm. I pull it back to see a crescent moon engraved into my hand.

"Just a precaution. Now come on God, let's get you to your mate."

It's been three days since Medusa was reunited with her familiar. Three days of stolen kisses and cuddles. Three days of trying to keep her away from the cabin and three days of us all trying to soak up any time she gives us. Sadly, all of that has been in passing or at night. Aside from our normal jobs we've all been busy working hard on her cabin.

Medusa on the other hand has been in helper mode as she helps Vera with her pups. Though Garen has insisted on her training in the morning with one of us while Vera is still resting, the moment training is done she gives us a quick kiss then quickly showers and eats before she is back to helping the Zark wolf with her pups.

"Why don't you take the day off, Medusa?" Taura suggests while we watch Medusa chug her coffee.

It's honestly impressive how she doesn't burn her mouth on the hot drink.

"But what if Vera or the pups need me?" She asks.

"Then I will help her, you need a break," Taura says as she takes Medusa's mug from her to refill it.

I swoop in. "That is a great idea Taura." I say as I wrap my arms around Medusa. "Do you want to see my bookstore?" I ask her, of course Kyrell picks that exact moment to walk into the kitchen.

"I think you mean our bookstore." He replies kissing Medusa on the cheek as he walks past her.

Rolling my eyes, I amend my invitation. "Excuse me, would you like to see our bookstore?" I ask as Taura walks back towards us with more coffee for my beautiful mate. Medusa steps out of my hold as she takes the cup, instantly taking a sip from it while I stand there waiting for her. I don't even want to take a breath in fear that she will say no.

"Okay." Medusa says, "Just let me get my shoes on." She says, before setting down her cup and rushing down the hall before I hear her footfalls head up the stairs.

"You think she is a little excited to go?" Kyrell asks with a chuckle.

"Not at all," I say with a smirk as I grab her cup of coffee walking over to the cupboard to pull out a larger cup with a lid. Pouring her drink in, I then add creamer and sugar before twisting the lid on. Moments later Medusa is walking back into the kitchen.

"Ready to go?" I ask her.

"I think so," she replies as she checks herself, making sure she has everything she needs.

"Good, now hold on," I tell her as I pull her into my arms. Traveling via shadows, we disappear from the house and reappear in front of my prized possession, Hidden Worlds.

CHAPTER 46
MEDUSA

My eyes soak in the three-story building, it has the same charm as the rest of the city with classic brick exterior ornate metal window trimmings, a large window takes up most of the wall on our left showing off displays of books. Giving off a magical vibe of wonder and adventure that any avid reader would desire to escape into.

"After you, my lady." Ace says as he holds the door open for me.

Smiling at him. "Well thank you, dear sir." I reply while stepping inside, only to end up stopping in my tracks. Thousands of books line the walls, shelves going up all the way to the ceiling, with three open floors above. A black spiral metal staircase sits in the back corner. The bottom level we are occupying is filled with unmatched chairs and tables. A fireplace sits to my right. It's magical, the place smells like the perfect blend of books, wood fire, coffee, and my guys.

"What do you think?" Ace asks, his breath tickling my skin.

"Can I live here?" I blurt out as I turn to face him, his black eyes are sparkling with silver flakes.

"If you want to, I'm sure we could figure something out." Ace says as he looks away, running his fingers through his hair. Tilting my head to one side as I study the expression on his face.

Stepping forward I turn his face gently with my hand. "I didn't really mean I wanted to live here, silly. I was just trying to say I love it so much I'd love to live here. But I'm happy at the cave castle." I reply, teasingly.

"Don't let Hades hear you call it that." He laughs as he wraps his arms around my waist.

"Only if he pisses me off." I tease, as I wrap my arms around his neck. He leans his head in closer.

"Just make sure I'm there to see it." Ace tells me as his scent of sandalwood and smoke wraps around me. I breathe it in. Before rising up on my toes, pressing my lips against his. My heart thumping wildly as I hear a sweet, soft moan leave his lips.

Ace's hands glide down my back, leaving a burning desire in their wake as his powerful hands slide over my ass. All my thoughts leave as I press my body closer to his. I literally can't get close enough to him. I'm loving every moment of this, even the way his scent mingles with mine. Ace scoops me up in his arms. My legs wrapping around his waist as he moves us, his lips never leaving mine. Soon I feel my back being pressed up against a bookshelf, I let out a small breathless whimper as he presses in against me. His restrained bulge pressing into my core. As his lips devour mine, pouring all his love and need into that kiss.

"Aren't you two a delicious sight?" Kyrell says as he stands by the front door, causing me to pull my lips from Ace's.

Ace smiles over at him as he lets me slide down gently. "It would have been better if you just let us continue." Ace admits.

"Oh, coffee," I say as I slip out of Ace's hold rushing over to Kyrell.

"Made by Raiden just for you. Besides sweetheart we can't properly work at a bookstore without our morning coffee," Kyrell says as he hands me a cup giving me a double dimple infused smile top off with a wink.

Oh, my stars.

"Alright, so you two going to give me the grand tour of this place before the customers file in?" I ask looking between my guys.

CHAPTER 47
OCTAVIUS

Closing my eyes, I take my time as I flow with the current, it's the moment of peace I need with so much change coming into our lives. It's so enticing to stay down here forever, no worries, just pure freedom. The only downfall is none of my mates can truly enjoy this part of my world with me for long. After checking on my ships I slowly make my way back to the house.

Surfacing, I smile as I see Hades standing there waiting for me.

"Is everything okay?" I ask as I walk over to the canopy where I left a towel and some extra clothes.

"Everything is fine, the cabin is finished." Hades replies.

"Finally," I say as I dry off my body.

"Get dressed, we have a few things to get from town before we show it to Medusa tonight."

"She will be thrilled." The damn woman gave me a heart attack when I saw she was missing from her bed last night. The sneaky girl tried to outsmart us and catch a glimpse of the place.

"Yes, no more patrolling at night to make sure she stays

away from it." Hades says with a chuckle just as I throw on my shirt.

"Alright I'm ready to go." Hades smiles and he opens a portal before we step through.

"I hope we didn't forget anything that she may need."

"We can always ask her and add onto it later," he replies as we enter downtown. Heading down the street until we reach The Dirty Brew.

"What brings you two in today?" I hear Othello say as he drops off some drinks to customers.

"Coffee and also wanting to see if you two are available to come over for dinner tonight before we show Medusa the cabin." Hades says.

"Does Medusa know?"

"No, Kyrell and Ace got her to leave the house today. So, I figured we'd surprise her with a family dinner before we finally let her see it."

"Oh, we know all about them luring her to her new favorite place." Raiden adds as he comes to stand next to Othello. "Kyrell stopped in to get a morning supply of coffee."

"Good she needs it; I have a feeling we'll have to set some boundaries for some down time ensuring that she has to put work aside." I say to the others as we walk over to the counter to order.

"What do you two want to drink?" Othello asks as he moves to the other side of the counter.

"I want a maple Spicer." I reply.

"Surprise me." Hades says making my mouth hit the ground. "Mister Up Tight and Things Must Be My Way, is letting someone else pick his coffee?"

"I didn't know what to order and I figured Othello or

Raiden wouldn't give me something terrible." He replies just as Nero bumps into him.

"Good morning slobber beast, I'm surprised you aren't hiding out with Medusa at the book shop." Hades says to Nero who immediately runs off disappearing through a dog door in the wall.

"I've never noticed that before." I say out loud.

"The dog door, yeah, we put it in the other day. That way if we are busy Nero can leave when he pleases instead of waiting for us to let him out." Raiden explains as he and Othello make our drinks.

"Well at least you know when he isn't here, he's with Medusa." I add.

"True." Othello says. "Lucky bastard." he mutters.

"What the fuck." Hades growls before opening a portal. "We will be back," he says, grabbing my arm before stepping through.

CHAPTER 48

ATTICUS

On all fours coughing up my lungs that are filled with seawater. Stupid warlock dropped me right into the ocean. Before instructing me to start swimming towards the beach and that once I am there, I will find Hades who can help me find my mate. Before he flies off on his broom laughing.

"How the fuck do people and creatures keep entering our wards? I swear after we deal with this guy, we are redoing everything!" I hear someone yelling in frustration from up the beach. I look up seeing a guy with blue flames for hair next to another guy who reminds of the pirates I'd see sailing around the oceans of our realm.

"Are you Hades?" I call out to him.

"Yes," Blue flames answers me.

"My name is Atticus, and I think you may know where my mate is."

"And who is your mate?" Hades asks.

"Her name is Medusa."

Hades eyes take me in, "We've been expecting you." he responds.

Standing up off the ground I plead with him. "Can you take me to her?"

"How about you get cleaned up first and then we'll take you to her." the other one says. "I'm Octavius by the way." he says just as Hades turns to head up the beach. It's then I notice the giant house built into the cliff side.

"Come on, let's get you inside." Octavius says as he turns to follow Hades inside. I jog to catch up with them.

"Are you guys' friends with Medusa?" I ask

"Something like that." he replies, making my insides freeze.

"I'll explain some of it on the way to the house. But don't punch me Hades doesn't like when his bonded get hurt. And take it from me you don't want to spend a night in Tartarus." Octavius calls over his shoulder.

What in the fates did Medusa get herself into.

CHAPTER 49
MEDUSA

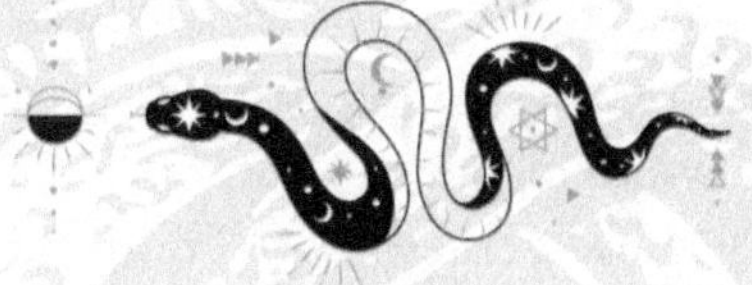

There had been no customers in the bookstore today, not that they complained. Ace and Kyrell were having way to much fun tormenting me all day with their flirty touches, stolen kisses, and fiery glances. Just one more stack of books for me, and I can leave for the house. My creature is pushing me hard to complete my bond with the guys. Of course, they don't make it easy to keep fighting her about why we needed to wait. Even now my resilience is slipping little by little. I'm so close to just stripping naked and pouring chocolate sauce on myself, just to get one of them to lick me.

"Medusa." I hear a familiar voice say.

Turning, my heart drops as I take in my golden god. "Atticus," I say as he rushes over to me, pulling me into his arms. I've missed him so much, I feel as though a piece of my soul just came home. I take a deep breath as I soak up his scent, the snakes on my head making fast on claiming him like they do the others.

He pulls away from me slightly. Medusa, is it really

you?" He asks as his eyes scan over my body looking for any injuries.

"It is. How are you here? Is your mother, okay?"

"That's a long story that I'll tell you later. And my mother is good." Atticus explains.

"Are you going to introduce us, Medusa?" I hear Kyrell ask. Before I can say anything, Atticus's golden wings burst from his back, wrapping me in tight.

"Atticus it's okay, they won't hurt me," I tell him. Pressing his forehead to mine while taking my hands in his.

"Who are they Medusa, I can see golden threads connecting you to them. It's the same one that I saw after Circe's spell wore off that connects you to me." His confession is something we will have to discuss later. But with him here it suddenly feels right to complete the bond with my mates.

"I'm their center, and yours as well," I tell him.

"Same old Medusa, not holding anything back, just jumping right in and giving out more than we all deserve." He whispers to me. Standing on my tiptoes I press my lips gently to his.

"It's who I am. Now let me introduce you to my other mates."

"Well, I already met Hades and Octavius." he grumbles.

"Perfect now you only have seven more introductions." I say walking over to my two other mates standing by Hades.

"Atticus, I'd like for you to meet Kyrell and Ace, they own this bookstore." I say just before Atticus gets tackled to the ground.

"Nero get off Atticus now, he's a friend." Chastising my favorite three headed pup. Nero pays me no heed, still holding Atticus down, his heads assessing my Sun God, with cautious snarls and curious eyes.

"Nero if you aren't nice you will have to sleep in your own bed tonight." I say, as Nero looks suitably chastised at my threat, looking over at me before backing off Atticus, and moving over to my side.

"Once he gets to know you, he will be your best friend." I explain, while scratching behind Nero's ears. Placating him for backing down and being a good boy.

"Let's get back to the house, he can meet the others while we make dinner." Hades says.

"Brilliant, can you make sure Othello and Raiden come as well?"

"Already taken care of, sweetheart." Hades replies as he pulls me into his arms pressing a kiss to my forehead.

"We will be home shortly, we just need to close the shop down." Kyrell adds as he and Ace step back from our group. I pull away from Hades, moving over to them, wrapping my arms around them both.

"Don't take too long." I tell them just as Hades opens a portal.

"Come on Nero, let's go home." I say as I get ready to step through.

CHAPTER 50
ATTICUS

Medusa has blossomed into the goddess I knew she always could be and more. One thing I know for sure, I'm never leaving her side again after we grab my mother and our things to bring them back here. To my surprise, Zakynthos is nothing like I imagined it to be, the creatures here are all so different yet they have a less barbaric way of living. Even their city center feels more like a community than Karpathos ever has. There everyone is always trying to prove they are better than the next god. Even the Fae and Dragonals rarely visited us anymore.

Everything here has me feeling new things I never felt before, attractions that leave me confused as my soul feels more complete than it ever had before.

Is this what it feels like to find your place in this life?

"I don't think I could eat another bite," I say, as I look at all the different foods still scattered across the table, tempting me to try them.

Medusa chuckles, "Cooper likes to cook." She says with a smile.

"This is nothing compared to what they've made for

parties," Taura says, as Medusa and her split another piece of chocolate cake.

"It's true, there is always so much food left over that we have to hand it out to guest as they leave." Octavius chimes in.

I smile as I grab Medusa's hand in mine, "Did you warn them that you live off of sweets and coffee." I tease her.

"Oh, we know how much she loves her bean juice," Raiden replies with a wink.

"It's also how she met Othello," Taura adds in.

"I'll admit this wasn't the life I had planned for us, but I can't deny how right it all feels." I admit to her, Medusa's purple eyes sparkling with love as she looks around the table. Sighing happily, she contentedly agrees with me.

"That it does."

"Well, I believe it's time to show Medusa her surprise." Hades says as he stands up and heads out of the room only to come back shortly with a long silk scarf as he moves to stand behind Medusa.

"You all better make sure I don't fall and land in a mud pit." she says as he places the scarf over her eyes.

"We would never allow it." Hades tells her as he ties the ends into a knot.

With one swift move he lifts Medusa out of her seat before setting her back on her feet before taking her small hand in his, interlacing their fingers.

Standing with the others we all file out the door following Medusa and Hades.

The path we follow isn't one I'd have taken if given a choice while exploring this property on my own. All the deadly strange looking plants and the dense tree and foliage on this path make my sense of danger go wild.

I am about to die of shock when Medusa holds out her

hand for a giant plant created from nightmares comes to her side. But in normal Medusa fashion even with a blindfold on she takes a moment to turn to the creature and talk with it before the damn thing licks her face.

"She's incredible," Kyrell says as he comes to stand next to me.

"That she is," I respond as I look over at him from the corner of my eye. The man is dangerous in the rightest way, not for the first time have I felt something more for him or one of the others. It's something I kept secret from Medusa, an attraction I found for both males and females. But these men have stirred something deep within me daring to let it out and make them mine.

"You keep lusting after us like that and you might get yourself into something you're not ready for yet god." Kyrell growls as he steps in closer to me and inhales.

"Fuck." I grumble.

A deep rumbling chuckle escapes his lips. "That's close enough of a description to what is to come." throwing an arm over my shoulder he pulls me along with me as we follow the others.

CHAPTER 51
KYRELL

"*Seems like we'll have to have a serious talk with our golden god.*" I say to the others.

"*I think it would be best that we should talk to him with Medusa tonight.*" Hades says.

"*Sounds good. He needs to know what all this means for himself, Medusa just needs to be there to support him.*" I add.

"*Sound like we have a plan.*" Hades says just as we arrive in front of the cabin. Taura helps to situate Medusa as we all gather in closer, I practically drag Atticus with me, the man is still so unsure of us all. Hades goes and unties the scarf from Medusa's eyes.

"How on the underworld did you build this all in only a few days?" she asks just as Taura grabs her hand.

"With magic of course, now come check it out." Taura tells her as they head inside. We all follow them. The moment I enter the place I can hear Medusa chatting excitedly with Taura.

"Look at this bedroom!! The bed could fit twenty

people. Why on earth would they build a bedroom here?" Medusa asks.

"For days we need to get away or when you need to stay here to take care of a creature." Octavius explains, "there is also a barn with stalls for different animals to stay in a food loft along with a glass terrarium for you."

"You guys really didn't have to do all that." she tells us as she starts going around giving out hugs and kisses. Once she has made a full circle her and Taura are off again as they explore the rest of the place. I start pulling out the fae wine we stashed here earlier, while Hades gets the fireplace lit. Lizzy the creepy dragon snap lays down on the ground next to Nero and Loki and Loki's mate Jezebel.

"Well, that is quite the sight." Raiden says as he nods towards the creature pile.

"I have a feeling it's just the start of what we should expect to see in our life with our goddess." I tell him dryly.

"True, be thankful that so far you've been lucky enough to avoid meeting Mixa." Atticus adds while leaning against the bar chair.

"Do I even want to know what a Mixa is?" Raiden asks.

"Mixa is a five-headed serpent that loves Medusa and absolutely loathes gods."

"It doesn't help that his owner is an imbecile. I hope Mixa ends up here far away from that owner, the dumb witted god thinks it's okay to keep Mixa locked up until there is a party or something he can show off Mixa and bug me for help." Medusa growls out as she comes over to where we are standing.

"When I go get my things I'll see if I can grab Mixa." Atticus promises Medusa. She just nods her head, I slide her a glass filled with fae wine.

"Thank you," she mutters to me.

"It is my pleasure to make sure you are always taken care of." I tell her as I grab her hand bringing it up to my lips and kiss it before keeping it hostage.

The rest of the evening we spent relaxing, played a few card games. Octavius played a few songs on his acoustic guitar that Taura and Medusa danced to. By the time we called it a night, we decided that we were all just going to stay here and head back to the other house in the morning.

"Keep your eyes closed, now use your senses to find me. Let your snakes guide you." I tell her before disappearing into the shadows. Circling Medusa I'm amazed by the creatures on her head as they follow my movements precisely. Like I instructed, Medusa lets them guide her right into my arms when she opens her eyes, I see they have changed. They are brighter purple, her pupils' slits.

"That was interesting," Medusa says.

"You did great, now are you ready to try bringing out your creature?" I ask her.

"Yes."

"Perfect, now just like you let them guide you, let your instincts guide you to her and she will do the rest."

Medusa's eyes flutter shut once more, she breathes in deep. I step back to give her a little room for the change to come over her. It's beautiful to see. The flow of magic seeps out of her, surrounding her like waves of water as it wraps around her before vanishing leaving her anew.

Scales line the top of her arms, covering her neck and

expanding down her chest under her tank top. I can only guess they cover her torso as well. Large golden scaled wings fan out behind her. Medusa's legs are now gone, replaced by a long-scaled tail with a mixture of green and gold scales. The snakes on her head are longer; and have now changed from their normal green coloring to reds, oranges, and golds – almost like they were dipped into the flames of a sunset.

"Wow," I say as I take a step closer to her.

Medusa's creature has a lure that draws me in like a moth to a flame. Whoever cursed her had no idea what they freed. The woman I was looking at now is a true Goddess.

"Do I look bad?" she asks, as her tail swishes back and forth in a smooth motion.

"Not at all. "I say, "You alone are breathtaking, but you in your full creature form is truly a sight to be seen. This must have been what the humans felt when they first saw the Gods and Goddesses. Because all I want to do is worship your mind, body, and soul." I tell Medusa as I pull her into my arms before crashing my lips against hers.

All reason fled, leaving only the madness of desire. Pulling back smiling as her breath is coming out in soft pants. The scent of our arousal filling the room as a powerful force fought for me to complete this bond between us. Closing my eyes, I draw in her sinful fragrance of spiced vanilla, jasmine, and raw untamed nights.

"I want nothing more than to indulge in you in every way," I tell her honestly, I don't want my little goddess thinking I am rejecting her. "I need to know everything about you, and you need to know everything about me before we complete our bond." Looking up into my eyes, her pupils enlarged.

"That sounds nice." She replies softly.

"Why don't we get you shifted back and go see how your mole friend is doing?"

"Breakfast is almost done," Atticus says as he steps into the room pausing when he sees Medusa in her full shifted form. "Dusa, you look..."

CHAPTER 53
MEDUSA

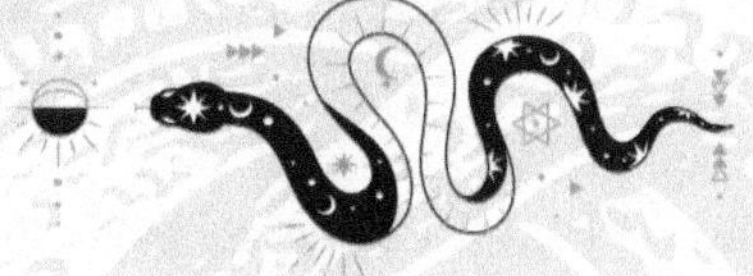

My heart is pounding, I can taste the rejection Atticus is about to give me. Before he runs off screaming.

"You don't have to say it," I whisper, closing my eyes not wanting to see the moment Atticus decides to reject me after seeing the monster I've become. Atticus steps closer gently cupping my face in his hands. As if I can't help it my eyes fly open. The look on his face would alone have my knees buckling, from the desire and devotion shining on his face.

"You look like a Goddess of the ancients," he tells me before pressing his lips gently to mine. "So can you actually fly with those pretty wings of yours, or are they just for looks?" He teases me just as his own golden wings burst from his back.

"I guess there is only one way to find out," I say. He smirks at me saucily.

"Do you even know how to get them to unfurl?"

"Of course, I do, I had wings before this." I remind him,

even if my other wings were not meant for flying and more for looks as they were made of vines and flowers.

"Yes, but those were more decorative than useful," he says with a chuckle.

I punch his arm teasingly. "Don't be mean." I chided him. Then like I would with any of my limbs, I think about what I want my wings to do. Instantly my wings unfold, spreading out behind me.

Fuck. They are heavy. Losing my balance, I begin to fall backwards. Panic shoots through me as I know this will hurt like no other. Instead, large arms catch me, pulling me back up. I look up to see Ace standing there smiling down at me.

"Maybe we should try it with legs till you have better control over your tail."

"That's probably a good idea," I reply, closing my eyes, calling upon the new shifting magic. I concentrate on just willing my tail to change back into legs. I soon hear a gasp and Atticus's soft whispers.

"Incredible," he murmurs. The awe in his voice, warming my heart and making me smile. When I open my eyes again, I see my tail is gone. And so are my pants.

"Atticus, can you grab my skirt over there for me?" I ask, thankfully I came prepared for when my pants would be ruined from my shifting.

"Of course," Atticus replies, walking over to the table I had placed my extra clothing on, grabbing the skirt he quickly brings it over to me.

"Thank you," I say, taking the skirt in hand before I turn my back to them both before stepping into the skirt.

"Okay, I'm ready to fly," I say to them as I turn back to find them both smiling.

"What?"

"Nothing," they say together.

CHAPTER 54
ATTICUS

Thirty minutes after having Medusa practice flapping her wings safely from the ground, Ace decided it was time for her to test them for real. To my surprise two large black wings appear on his back just before he grabs Medusa from behind while I wait ready from the ground. He flies up to the tall ceiling of the training room.

"You ready to give this a try, little goddess?" Ace asks Medusa.

"More than ready," she replies loud enough for me to hear, knowing she has dreamt about flying her whole life. When he is high enough, Ace says something to her, Medusa nods her head before he lets her go.

"Perfect, beautiful, keep them open like that, "He flies above her, telling her what to do while I continue to wait on the ground. Watching her like a hawk for any signs of her struggling, just when I'm about to fly up and catch her, her wings finally catch the air as she glides past me, giggling.

I whistle out at her before I fly into the air, only to end up colliding with Ace. He must have not seen me as he was watching, as proudly as I was, Medusa's first flight. Landing in a heap of wings and body parts, I call my wings back into me. I hear a small soft giggle.

"Are you guys, okay?" Medusa asks.

"I will be if you kiss me where it hurts," I say to her, while pouting out my lips.

"And where does it hurt?" she asks.

"Everywhere."

"If he gets kisses everywhere, it's only fair I do too." Ace says as he pushes me off me.

"Breakfast is ready," Everett says as he walks into the room. Medusa smiles as she walks over to him, retracting her wings like a pro.

"Oh, good I'm starving." She says as she looks over at us giving me the most sinful look I have ever seen on her face. Everett stills as he must have caught her double meaning like we did, cursing under his breath Ace jumps to his feet.

"You still owe me kisses," I shout.

Medusa winks at us all before rushing out of the room, her musical laugh echoing back to us. I rush to my feet before I run after her. I hear two more sets of footsteps behind me as I follow her scent leading outside. I stop in the doorway to the back patio, as she waves at me from her seat between Kyrell and Garen. Ace and Everett stand behind me, cursing our little minx. My eyes never leave hers. I take the seat directly across from Medusa, a plan forming in my mind.

I load my plate up with food and make sure to grab some grapes and strawberries. With a smirk, I take one of the ripe berries, twirling my tongue around the tip. Medusa's heady scent flitters towards me as I hold her focus, I suck the tip into my mouth before pulling it out with a pop. Medusa's eyes are now fully dilated, her scent filling the air.

"God damn, please tell me you all aren't about to have an orgy for breakfast," Taura says, breaking the spell we all were under. Blush covers Medusa's face as she looks down at her plate before her eyes flutter to look up at me from under her long lashes.

"Not today," I reply as I bite into the strawberry.

CHAPTER 55
MEDUSA

I am finally getting the hang of portal travel. It's extremely useful, especially when I want to get somewhere quickly. With all the guys in twos behind me. Taura and I walk into the animal sanctuary. The woman at the front desk smiles at me.

"I was hoping you were coming in today." she says. I smile back as I see a nameplate on the desk that reads Lilura, head healer at Eden Animal Sanctuary.

"Is Nelson, okay?" She looks at me strangely, "I mean the mole?" I corrected myself, as I realized that I never told anyone that his name was Nelson. Lilura smiles up at me like she thinks I'm adorable for naming a mole.

"Yes, Nelson is okay. Would you like to see him?"

"Yes," I say, a little too fast. "I mean, yes please." Atticus wraps an arm around my shoulder comfortingly.

"She has a gift for animals and tends to care a great deal for them." He explains.

"I understand completely. Follow me, fellow-creature lover, and I'll show you the way to Nelson." Lilura says.

Wasting no time, I slip out of Atticus's hold and follow

239

her through the doors. The sound of footsteps behind me increases as the guys and Taura follow me. Something so simple as this makes me smile, as they all seem to care greatly, as I do. Or at least they want to help support me in some small way. Whatever their reasons for coming with me to check on this creature, it makes my heart swell. We step into a room that resembles a forest, in the center is a glass square filled with dirt on top, lays a dome. I step closer, smiling when I see Nelson snuggled up in a ball inside the dome.

"Nelson should be ready to return to his home in a few days. He was lucky you found him when you did, if it had been any longer, I'm afraid he wouldn't have made it." Lilura explains to us.

"Do you have any idea what might have caused his injury?" I ask. Lilura stands next to me, pausing to consider my question carefully before she gives me an answer.

"We don't. It honestly could have been caused by multiple things, a sharp rock is what we are guessing. It is possible that it could have been another animal, even a sharp tree root." She tells me.

"Thank you," I tell her as I look at Nelson one last time. "I will be back for you in a couple of days, Nelson," I say before we all leave back out the way we came in. Once back outside we start walking home, enjoying the nice day as we head towards The Dirty Brew to meet Ace who snuck out to get our orders placed.

As we step inside the cafe, Ace waves over to us. I smile when I see Othello sitting at the booth with him, along with Nero and Raiden. Ace stands up so I can slide into the booth.

"Is he doing, okay?" Othello asks as he settles his arm over my shoulders.

"He is, Lilura the head healer said I'd be able to bring him back home in a few days."

"That is good," Othello says.

"So, Medusa, Othello and I have already talked it over with the others, but we've decided to move in with all of you at the cave castle." Raiden tells me.

"Seriously?" I ask biting my lip to keep from squealing.

"Seriously, next week we'll build a brewing barn and move once that is completed."

"It will be the best birthday gift ever to be with you all in one place." I say out loud.

"Birthday?"

"When is your birthday, Medusa?"

"October 31st, La Notte delle Streghe," I reply.

"Then we will have to celebrate," Taura says as she practically pushes Raiden and Othello out of the way as she climbs over them and settles in next to me.

"We could go to The Bent Broom." I say.

"Perfect, maybe we can add in some surprise stripper to pop out of your cake." Taura adds as she starts writing down a list of things she will need.

"Is this normal?" I whisper over to Cooper who just laughs at my expense.

"Very normal." Taura replies to me.

CHAPTER 56
OTHELLO

I smile watching our mate while our new sister gives her a lecture on why there must be a stripper in her cake to pop out of it.

"Think Taura would be mad if we killed the stripper if he comes near our mate?" Raiden asks me as we make another round of drinks for our family.

"Possibly maybe we can talk her into making sure we put Hades in the cake." I joke while imagining the tightass popping out of the cake mad as hell because he was forced into it.

Hahaha, "I'm sure that could be arranged." Octavius answers startling me, fucking sneaky kraken.

"How on earth do you move so quietly?" Raiden asks, as he wipes off his shirt. Apparently, I wasn't the only one startled.

"I just came over to tell you we think after we let Taura throw her extravagant birthday bash we will all whisk Medusa away to the cabin and complete our bond."

"Now that's a plan I can get on board with," I reply. "What about you Raiden?"

"It's all I've been dreaming about since she first walked into that bar." Raiden admits.

"As long as it's what she wants then we are all in." I tell Octavius.

"Of course, we would never push our girl to do anything she didn't want to." Octavius replies as we all look over to the booth filled with our loves. Quickly we finish up the drinks before placing them on trays and head back over to the table, somehow, they got one of the metal glasses. Kyrell and Atticus are sitting across from each other as they try to bounce coins into it. When Kyrell gets his in, he screams while tossing his arms in the air, instantly Hades replaces Atticus.

"Are you ready to take on the king?" he asks Kyrell. Grinning a wolfish grin Kyrell is deliberately goading him.

"Always." Kyrell replies as they start again.

"Here you go Medusa," I say as I hand her a drink. While Hades and Kyrell keep playing, we pass around everyone's drinks, setting theirs off to the side, so they don't knock them over.

"They are completely bonkers." Raiden whispers to me.

"But we wouldn't want it any other way." I reply just as Nero comes running in through his dog door followed by Lizzy who gets stuck.

"Fuck, Lizzy you won't fit through there." Medusa screams as she jumps over the back of the booth.

"See bonkers." Raiden says with a laugh as we watch Medusa talk to the plant who I'm pretty sure thinks it's a dog.

CHAPTER 57

MEDUSA

I feel arms wrap around my stomach pulling me against a strong chest. The scent of sunshine and sweet citrus fills the space around me.

"I've got a surprise for you." Atticus whispers against my ear, his warm breath tickling my neck.

Spinning in his arms I stand up on my tiptoes to press a kiss to his lips. Like every time I kiss one of the guys, something I mean to just be sweet turns into a frenzy. Soon my back is pressed against the door, and I'm being hauled up into his arms. My legs wrap around his waist as I pull him in closer to me. A moan slipping out of my lips. By some miracle, Atticus pulls his lips from me, but I don't care. I just start kissing down his neck, nibbling as I go.

"Medusa you need to stop, or I'll end up fucking you against this door." He tells me.

"I'm game." I mumble as I continue my attack on his neck. His chuckle echoes through the room as I feel him let go of my thighs letting my body slide against his as I make my way back to the ground. The moment my feet hit the ground Atticus takes my hand in his leading me out the side door from the front room.

We take the side path leading into the garden and end up back at the pond next to where the start of my cabin is. I stop as I see a blanket with many pillows set up on the grass and a few floating lanterns dispersed through the trees surrounding us.

"I had a little help from the others." Atticus says as he guides me over to the blanket. I sit down smiling as I see two wine glasses and a bottle of fae wine sitting next to a picnic basket.

"Didn't eat enough at dinner?" I ask Atticus as I kneel and go for the basket to see what is inside. Atticus places his hand on mine stopping me from opening it.

"It's for dessert but I figured we'd start with some fae wine."

"Trying to get me drunk already?" I tease.

"Of course, since the last time we were alone together I did promise you a night of drinking, eating too many sweets and a sexy god to fuck." He says with a wink.

"Oh, and who is this sexy God you have found for me to fuck?" I ask, trying not to laugh.

"Me." He says just as his lips connect with mine while his hands grab hold of my waist hauling me into his lap so that I am now straddling his waist. I'm thankful I wore a skirt today with two high slits on each side. Making this position very appealing to my throbbing core as I grind down on Atticus' hard length. Sparks fly across my skin, and I grind against him again. A breathy moan slipping out of my lips as his fingers brush across my sensitive nub. Pulling away Atticus has a devilish grin spreading across his lips.

"You naughty minx. You haven't been wearing any

underwear?" I grind into his fingers, as he continues to play with me.

"The slits go up too high to wear any." I admit as I start pulling at his shirt. He chuckles at my attempt to get him naked.

"Why don't we have some wine first then I'll let you have your way with me." He says. I cross my arms pouting at him.

"Fine but I'm sitting right here." I grumble at him.

"Like I'd let you move from my lap." He mutters under his breath as he opens the bottle of fae wine. Filling the glasses to the brim he hands me one. "I love you Medusa." Atticus says as he clicks his glass against mine and downing his glass. I drink my own glass tossing it aside, I press my lips back to his.

"I love you too Atticus." I admit to him before I devour his lips, grinding back down on him. Atticus pulls back to dispose of his shirt before helping me out of mine. His head dips down sucking my nipple into his mouth.

"Atticus, I need you in me." I whimper out. Without releasing my tit, he flips our positions so that I am laying on my back. His fingers easing in and out of my opening.

"So wet for me?" He groans out before adding another finger into me. I'm so close as I feel a pressure growing inside of me. Atticus seemed to read my thoughts curling his fingers in a come here motion hitting my sweet spot sending me right over the top. My walls constrict around his fingers as I ride out the waves of pleasure.

Atticus pulls out his fingers making my eyes fly open only to be greeted with a sinful sight of him stripping out of his pants. Sitting up I watched as he unbuttons and painfully slowly pulls them down over his hips exposing more of his v that leads to the holy stick. When he finally freed his cock, I'm kneeling up not even waiting for him to take off his pants all the way I wrap my hand around his thick hard length. Slowly I rubbed my finger over the tip spreading the precum that was leaking out.

"Medusa!" He growled out as a warning, but I wasn't wasting this opportunity to taste him. I brought my lips towards his tip letting in part my lips running my tongue over the tip licking up his sweetness before gliding my tongue down his length. He wasn't as long as Hades, but his girth was incredible. I couldn't wait to ride it.

"Baby you're killing me." He moaned out. Smiling, I started bobbing my head as I took more of him into my mouth. I felt his hand push on my head moving me faster as he fucks my mouth.

"Fuck, your mouth feels so good Medusa." I hummed in reply only to be granted with a growled fuck.

"Baby I want to be inside of you." Slowly I pull back my mouth making a pop sound as his punishment springs free of its clutches. Atticus was back on me the tip pressing against my entrance as he not only kissed my lips but fucked them with his mouth. His tongue swirling with mine as he tasted himself.

With one thrust he buried himself in me, filling me all the way up, my soaking wet cunt feeling deliciously full. Giving me only a moment to adjust to his size before pounding into my sweet cunt.

The pressure of an orgasm building once again and fast. Soon I was at his mercy as my skin grew scorching hot and sensitive wherever his body touched mine. That mixed with the feeling in my pussy Atticus's cock was creating, it felt like too much. And yet although I was straining to process the sensations swimming through my body, I didn't want it to end.

"Don't worry my love, we have all night." Atticus whispered in my ear before biting down on my neck making my world explode in an epic orgasmic way. Feeling our mate bond snap into place, I feel content.

CHAPTER 58
OCTAVIUS

Atticus left this morning with a promise of returning soon with his mother. We'd later set up a portal to bring more of their things here that they couldn't carry. Medusa on the other hand was a little mopey with not having Atticus here.

Medusa busied herself with helping Vera who was moving into the guest suite that Medusa had been in as we moved her things down to our suite that had fourteen rooms and one main mating suite, that way if we needed to have a break from the others, we could but mostly they just held our clothes. "I think I'm going to take Medusa to see my cave," I tell the others as we carry another box of Medusa's things, we've been secretly buying for her down from the hidden room we've been working on for her.

"I think it will be good for her to get out." Hades says as he holds open the door for her room. With Taura taking charge of organizing Medusa's closet I set off to find our beautiful goddess.

No one is better at distracting a woman than me. Usually, it involved a lot of rum and a skinny dipping in the ocean, but that was the old me. The wild me, the Kraken without his captain. Now I had Medusa, and even though I would love nothing more than to get her naked with me in the ocean, this was more to cheer her up. My Kraken was practically yanking me by the tentacles. He was so excited for her to see him in all of his glorious self.

With Vera's help it didn't take me long to convince Medusa, leading her downstairs Taura handed her a swimsuit and dress before slamming the door in her face. I let her use my room to change.

"Trust me, this is just what we both need," I tell Medusa as I lead her down to the beach.

"How can swimming in the ocean be what I need?"

"Well for one, it will help you relax, love. For two, I can show you, my creature, he's been begging to come out and meet you." I tell her as we stroll towards the water lapping at the sand. My kraken and I are in complete agreement, she is the gem in my sea. I willingly give her the key to my heart. She is the captain of my ship. The north star that will always lead me home.

"Really?" She asks, with her face lighting up.

"I would never lie to you, love. Now, strip out of that pretty dress." I tell her as I strip out of my own clothes. Medusa smiles as she sets her bag down on the table under the canopy, kicking off her sandals as she pulls the dress up overhead. Leaving her in a black bikini. I feel like it's my birthday, as Medusa looks like the most delicious snack.

"You'll stay with me the whole time, right?" she asks.

"I promise, love," I tell as I grab her hand in mine. Sucking in a deep breath she nods as we walk into the water together. I only let go of her hand when we reach the deep water so we can swim.

"I'm going to dive under and shift. It may take a few minutes," I explain to Medusa.

Giving her a quick kiss before diving under the clear blue water. I look back up at her, seeing her smile down at me. I turn my head and swim for a little longer before calling upon my creature, letting the change flow over me. My shifting is painless as my bones and skin stretch and grow with my creature reforming my whole being. My skin changes to various shades of blues and green. Though, if needed, I can change my skin to blend in with my surroundings.

When I finally do resurface it is as my creature, Medusa looks over me with wonder. I hold out a tentacle for her to examine. I shiver as she runs her soft hands over my sensitive skin as I bring another tentacle underneath my mate so she can rest on it while she explores me and not have to worry about trying to keep herself floating at the same time. After a few minutes, Medusa looks up at me, smiling, before diving into the water. Surprising me as she swims closer to my eye.

"Care to take a swim with me, my mighty Kraken?" She asks into my mind, making my three hearts burst with joy.

"I know a place but it's a bit of a swim, so if you want, you can ride me while I swim," I tell her. Medusa nods her head and swims over to my body where she nestles herself close to me. I raise us closer to the surface so all she will need to do is stand to get more air into her lungs.

Once I know she is settled into place, I take off swimming to my secret cave. With me swimming in my Kraken form it will only take ten minutes to reach. It's where I have kept my favorite ships from my days as a pirate king. Many treasure hunters and greedy monsters would die to see just one of my ships that lay hidden from the world.

Let alone the mountains of gold and gems I've gathered or stolen from sunken ships.

On occasion, I bring the guys here and Coop casts a spell so we can sail on one of the ships enjoying the open ocean and each other. I start to slow down as we get closer to the entrance, which lies hidden.

"We're going to have to dive under to get to the entrance," I warn Medusa before diving down deep below the waves, swimming to the secret entrance. Wrapping a tentacle around Medusa, I slide us both through the entrance before I place her gently on my most treasured ship: The Jeweled Serpent. Once I know she is safely on the boat, I shift back to my humanoid form before climbing up the rope ladder and joining her on the deck. Medusa takes me in as she stands there, looking so tempting, a very long-awaited wet dream of mine. One that I and the others were close to giving up on.

"So, my mighty Kraken Captain, are you going to show me around this stunning ship or are we just going to stand here staring at each other while you try to melt my swimsuit off with your eyes?" Medusa asks while staring at my member that is standing at her attention between my legs. Standing more proudly, I strike a pose, giving her a better look at all of me in my naked form.

"Are you sure about that love? You want a tour of the ship, or would you rather explore me?"

"Maybe I wanted to find a bed to explore you on." She replies as she steps towards me, her hips swaying with every step.

All I see is red, as I meet her, lifting her up into my arms as I press her back into the mast, my lips descend down on hers. I pour everything I have ever felt for her into that kiss, my desire, my love, my soul. I was offering Medusa my heart on a platter for her to do as she pleased with it, as long as it meant I got to be by her side. I slipped my tongue into her mouth, she gasped as it splits and twirls around hers, I fuck her mouth, show her everything I could be doing to her in other parts. With a wicked thought, I pulled back, letting my mouth wander from hers, tracing the contour of her throat.

"Medusa, have you ever had a man pleasure you with his mouth while swimming?" I ask her.

"Are you volunteering?" she asks with a moan, and I suck on her neck. I pull away, looking into her eyes.

"I am." I reply with a smirk before I toss her over my shoulder and run for the edge of the boat, jumping off into the warm water below.

"Octavius," Medusa screams my name, causing me to laugh. With a wave of my hand water catches us in its grasp before setting us gently down in the shallow waters at the edge of my treasured beach. Setting her down in the water, I smile down at her.

"First things first, love, you need to lose that bikini." I tell her before I kneel in front of her. I gently grab each of her knees in my hands, spreading her legs apart before I drag her up into my arms. Placing my lips back on hers, I untie the bottoms, pulling them free from her body before untying the top. Once she was fully bare to me, I pull her into my arms before wading us out a little further into the water.

When I was satisfied with the depth I dipped my head below the water, scraping my teeth on her inner thigh as I grasped them in my hands, pulling them apart and bringing her center to my mouth. Even the water couldn't wash away the scent of her arousal.

I dart my tongue between her lips, my dual tongue

probing and exploring her depths. Soon Medusa was moving her hips in time with my tongue, encouraging me, whispering more. She weaves her fingers through my hair as my tongue lashes inside her, working her opening. With one last bold swipe of my tongue, it sent her spinning into pleasures' arms. Resurfacing, I guide us back to the edge of the water. I flip us so that I am the one lying in the black sand and gold while I lift Medusa onto my thick ribbed head.

"Just tell me to stop, and I will," I tell her.

"Don't you dare stop," she replies as she stares into my eyes, slowly easing herself down, taking me in. Medusa moans as the scale-like textures strewn throughout my shaft slides in, filling her completely. She stretches and melts around me before she starts grinding atop of me, moving faster. I meet her movements with my own, I grasp her hips as I pick up our pace.

"Octavius, I need more." She begs before I flip our positions and place her on her hands and knees, before I plunge into her, driving my cock deep into her soaked lips. The cave echoes with the sound of our moans and skin slapping as we move together as one. I dip my hand between her legs, finding her clit with one swipe of my fingers. Medusa comes hard, the power of her orgasm has my manhood dancing and coating her with my sperm.

"Ready for round two?" She asks as I pull out of her.

"Of course, love," I reply, before spinning her in my arms and kissing her.

CHAPTER 59

ATTICUS

The putrid scent of dark magic fills the air, a smell that I know all too well. I spent the last five years trapped in its embrace, and now I am willingly walking into the trap that awaits me on the other side of the door. I have no choice, who knows what things she could be doing to my mother.

"Welcome home, Atticus." Circe says as I step into the house.

"Where is my mother?" I ask her.

"She is safe. And she will remain safe, as long as you do what you are told, my pet." Circe says with a wicked grin. "Now, why don't you take a seat and I'll get you a drink." I grind my teeth and I do as I'm told. "Good boy." She coos at me before heading into the kitchen just as Zeus joins us from the shadows. He has a hold of my mother with a dagger resting against her neck.

"Let her go." I say.

A malicious smile crests Zeus' face. "Oh no son, you do not give me the orders here. I can end your mother with a swift slice. Now you will do as I say. Circe has made you both a sweet potion that you will take without a fight, or we'll have to do it the hard way." he says as he nods to where she is standing. Circe pricks her finger; she lets three drops of blood fall into it, one of the glasses making the potion turn pink. She carries the other over to Zeus.

"Don't move Sumerian I'd hate to end you before we have our fun." He tells my mother before he releases her for a moment so Circe can prick his finger. Just like she did before three drops of blood drip into the other glass before it turns from blue to pink.

"Drink up." He says handing the glass to my mother. She looks my way, before glaring up at the king and grabbing the glass and downing the contents.

"Your turn Atticus." Circe says as she walks towards me.

"Why do you hate her so much?" I ask, needing to know what the end game was.

"Power. I want her vast wells of power. These other gods have been fooled by her. Not me, I could smell all the power hiding deep within her. Now that she is a monster, we can finally strip it from her." Zeus says as he smiles, knowing I have no choice here.

"Now drink up my pet," Circe says, holding out the glass. Glaring at her, letting her see the hatred I have for her before I press the cup to my lips and tilt my head back to drink the potion and her blood.

"*Medusa please forgive me.*" I send my fleeting thoughts out into the universe hoping she'll hear them even with the distance in our bond. Instantly I feel my bond with Medusa closing off from me, replaced by an unnatural one to Circe. A burning need to please her fills me and soon my craving for Medusa is completely gone. Zeus and my mother vanish but at this moment I don't care. My world revolves around one woman now, Circe. I stand, making my way over to her.

"Welcome back, my love, I've missed you." She says to me as she stands snapping her finger, making all of her clothes disappear. A delicious shudder shoots through me at the thought of her, mindlessly consuming my body. I was powerless to resist her foreign charm as she sat back down on the couch, spreading her legs apart, propping her feet on the table, giving me a view of her luscious lips. Teasing me as she slid a finger inside her with one hand, while her other flicked and pulled on her nipple.

"You like what you see, my love?" She asks as she adds another finger into her pussy.

"Yes, my goddess," I say to her. As her heady scent fills my lungs, my need to taste her grows.

"Do you want a taste?" She asks.

"Yes, my goddess."

"Then come here and taste me. Come pleasure your goddess and let me reclaim you as mine, my pet."

In an instant, I kneel, before removing her fingers. I suck them into my mouth, tasting her juices. Once I've licked her fingers clean, I dip my head down as I explored her with my tongue. I enjoy the sounds she makes as my tongue lashes inside her, working her opening. While Circe arches into me as I eat her, my mouth never stops working her center.

Circe entwines her fingers through my hair as she starts riding my face, chasing her orgasm. Knowing she was close I reach up with my hand, flicking her clit, in a matter of seconds, she is screaming out my name as I drink up every drop of her juice, and she releases my hair. I kiss my way up her body.

My teeth scrape against her shoulder, before I lean over,

our mouths meeting, tongues dancing with each other as she tastes herself. I flip her quickly, her knees on the cushion with her hands on the back. She looks over at me as I plunge my cock ruthlessly into her center.

"Yes, Atticus fuck me. Claim me as yours." She screams as I pick up the pace.

CHAPTER 60
MEDUSA

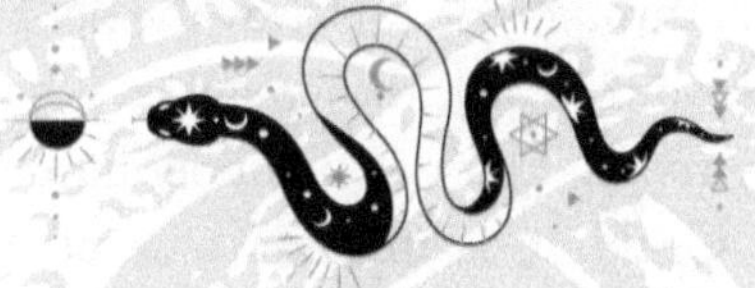

Swimming with Octavius was a pastime I could do every day. It was exactly what I needed today. Atticus leaving earlier had triggered insecurities I didn't know I still had. I couldn't help the foreboding I felt. I always wanted to be true to myself, but will they still love me if I show the struggles that lie in the shadows of my soul?

I had been feeling lost drowning in uncertainty until Octavius had dragged me to the ocean and pulled me out of my head. I could have sworn I felt Atticus pleading for forgiveness and help, but that was probably my own fears and insecurities plaguing me. So, I'd been grateful to Octavius for so thoroughly distracting me from my fears and misery.

"Hurry and get ready Medusa, and then we will stop by The Dirty Brew before we head over to my shop," Taura shouts from the living room.

"I just need to shower and change," I reply as I quickly run down the stairs to our level where all my mates and I will stay.

Opening the door to my new room, I freeze in place as I

see the window is open. That's not the issue though, it's the impossibly large raven sitting on my bedpost. Its eyes are blood red, and its mind is blocked. I can't sense its emotions. It feels dangerous. Something isn't right about this situation. Cautiously I walk backward slowly to the door. Before I even get a limb through the doorway the door slams shut.

"Who are you?" I ask the creature. The smell of dark magic fills my room. The raven is now hidden in a swirl of black smoke. Cackling is my first clue of who I am now facing. Circe steps out of the smoke.

"You really should have died in the ocean Medusa, it would have made this whole situation a lot less painful for you."

"Sorry to disappoint you Circe. What do you want?" I ask as I call my own magic forward. She smiles maliciously at me, her eyes glittering with hate and envy.

"Aside from Atticus, who by the way sends his regrets, he couldn't be here to tell you that we've mated in person. But that won't matter for long, as you will soon be a permanent resident in the underworld."

"You lie. Atticus would never mate with you freely." I shout as my hair hisses.

"Oh, but he did Medusa. In a sad attempt to protect his mother, sad how easy he is to manipulate. He is lucky he is such a good fuck."

"Fuck you, you rapist piece of shit!" I shout before lunging at her. I smile as I land a hit to her once-perfect nose. Blood trickles down and she wipes the flowing liquid from her face looking down at it. I move again while she is still staring down at her fingers.

"You bitch." She shouts before snapping her fingers. I should have known she was planning something. As I am suddenly tackled to the ground, sitting on my chest is

Atticus. He wraps his hands around my throat. His eyes are glazed, none of his familiar spark shines in them. They are dull and lifeless. My soul knows that this isn't truly him I am staring at. Our connection still there in my heart has been completely wiped out in his. Black dots are starting to dance in my vision. But even with Atticus so spelled I can't help but try to reach out to him. To my mate.

"Atticus, I forgive you," I tell him knowing that once he is free from Circe's spell the guilt of whatever happens to me will wrap its ugly self around his heart. I know now that his plea was real and not just a figment of the pain at being separated from our bond. He had been desperately seeking to communicate with me, even from such a distance. Praying I would recognize the difference between the true Atticus and whatever dark magic Circe had ensnared him with.

Hopefully when he frees himself, he remembers this moment, and will know that I understood this truly wasn't him. I had heard his desperate plea, but even without it I would have known. The man currently draining my lifeforce, could never be mistaken for the sweet, loving man I had always known. Dark magic could not replicate the purity of our love in our unbroken bond.

As the darkness of eternal rest pulls me ever so slowly into its embrace, I am no longer fighting it. Surprisingly I find I am more than happy to go. I have known love, love deeper and truer than I ever expected. Love so strong, that even death itself would not dare to destroy it. Our bonds are too strong and there is pure magic in that. Just before the embrace of death completely envelops me, I see a gleam in Atticus' eyes.

To be continued.......

GLOSSARY

- Medusa - (Me-doo-sa) - Goddess of nature & creatures/cursed and is now also a gorgon shifter
- Atticus - (At-ti-cus) - God of sun and moon
- Hades - (Ha-d-es) - King of the Underworld
- Octavius - (Oc-ta-vi-us) - Kraken - Shapeshifter
- Kyrell - (Ky-rail) - Grimmarg - Shapeshifter
- Garen - (Gar-en) - Kipin - Shapeshifter
- Othello - (O-th-el-o) - Necromancer
- Raiden - (R-ay-den) - Zombie
- Ace - (A-ce) - Boogeyman - Shadow creature
- Cooper - (Coo-p-er) - Warlock
- Everett - (Ev-er-et) - Gargoyle
- Taura - (T-a-u-er-a) - Witch
- Sumerian - (Sum-er-an) - Goddess of the Moon and Stars
- Vera - (V-air-a) - Zark Wolf-Shifter

MEDUSA'S FAMILIAR, PETS AND CREATURES THAT SHE TAKES CARE OF OR MAKE AN APPEARANCE

- Loki- Giant Tortoise - (Medusa's familiar)
- Jezebel - Giant Tortoise - Loki's mate
- Lulu - Aequilla
- Nelson - Mole
- Lizzy - Snap Dragon Hydnora - (dragon snap for short) giant meat-eating plant that can uproot itself and move, using its roots as feet to walk. (Piranha plant or, in real life, also known as a Hydnora Africana)
- Nero - Giant three-headed dog - (Othello's familiar)
- Mixa - Five-headed serpent
- Pancake - Wolpertinger - bunny with wings and horns

REALMS/ISLANDS

Loreath Realm

- Zakynthos (Zak-in-those) - Velaris Island - all are welcome
- Karpathos (Kar-path-os) - Elysian Island - Evercrest Forest - only elite allowed
- Aequreal (Auq-u-real) - Oceania Island - Pearlsea Resort
- Velaris (Vel-ar-is) - Umbra Island - shadow island

- Draco (Dra-co) - Empyrean Island - dragon shifters and alike monsters - keep to themselves for now
- Synodic (syn-o-dick) - Vampires and other blood-driven monsters
- Lucelence (Lu-ce-l-en-ce) - Fae Island - is split into 4 different kingdoms- fall, winter, spring, and summer.
- Anodyne - (an-o-dine) - Gorgon/ harpys
- Goetic (Go-e-tick) - Goblins and alike creatures
- Epochal (E-poch-al) - Two islands - griffins
- Tilleul (Til-ul) - Neamon island
- Mullistus (Mull-is-tus) - Selkies
- Henotic (He-no-tic) - Water creatures
- Eramnesia (Er-am-nes-a) Healer Island - temple and small town there, if they choose, all choose to all healers from each kind are allowed to come and train or grow their gifts, also after completing training they are allowed to return and take some of the special plants or herbs they grow on the island.
- Tectus (tec-tus)
- Tartius (tar-ch-us) - [hidden deep on this island] - Island of souls- only Hades and those he allows can step foot here, Zeus and Poseidon are of course granted because of blood relation, though Hades set traps to keep Zeus from releasing titans again.
- Lito Island (Li-to) - Nymph Island
- Poiesis Island (Poi-se-sis) - Kraken Island - Octavius's Island where he keeps his boats and treasure.

NOTE TO THE READERS

In Chapter 34- when Octavius sings- listen to *Come With Me Now* by **The Kongos**.

Also, if you want to listen to a playlist that goes with the whole book check out my writing playlist on Spotify - Medusa's Curse

TO MY INCREDIBLE TEAM

Thank You To my whole team...... We did it! No, I'm serious, Medusa is finished, well the first book.

I want to say a huge thank you to everyone who ever helped me with my book at any stage of my writing and supported me when I had moments of not being able to continue on with my difficult writing adventure of Medusa's Curse.

Thank you, Charley, for taking me in and also laying down the law so that I would finally finish this story. It's come a long way from where I started but thank you so much for giving me the extra push and taking care of all the other stuff while I focused on writing. I know our journey between PA and author is just beginning but you have already done so much for me. Thank you.

I want to give a special shout out to Jade Thorn for helping me write my blurb and talking over a few ideas while I was still finding this story's way.

Now I can't forget my Alpha's or say thank you enough ladies so much for all your help Ashley and Beth! You two are so incredibly amazing and kept me from tossing in the towel. You helped me transform Medusa's Curse from an okay story to one that I hope no one forgets.

I want to give a shout-out to my Beta's thank you all so much for adding your special flavor to the book.

Thank you, Maria, for taking the wheel and chance and helping me finish the book when me and my alphas hit our tap-out point. You are one truly special and talented editor, and I can't thank you or the rest of my team enough for all you did for me and my book.

I want to give a huge thank you to DAZED Designs for my beautiful cover. I swear with every new cover you keep outdoing yourself and I find myself in love with each one. I can't wait for the rest of the world to see all the others you have created for the upcoming books.

I also want to thank you for the incredible formatting and designs.

To my husband, thank you for being so patient with me as I ignored the house and wrote my book and for not hiding my computer while I did that. Love you.

Lastly, I would like to thank my readers, you all are so supportive and have waited so long for this book. I'm so thrilled to finally give you the long-awaited story of Medusa and her mates. I hope you all enjoy the rewrite I have done for the start of this series.

About the Author

Josslyn Leach is a why choose paranormal romance author.

She lives in the middle of a beautiful desert with her husband, two kids, and two dogs.

She loves reading, drawing, painting, doodling, studying apothecary, and herbology, along with many other things.

When she isn't home you can find her living out of a tent with her family in the woods as they explore the mountains and collect rocks.

She found her love for reading and telling stories at a young age, with a wild amount of imagination that seemed to only grow as she got older. She finds her inspiration from dreams and the voices in her head that constantly declare their stories must be told.

She recently pulled all her books down, so she could add all the magical gems of inspiration into them that she wasn't able to the first-time round. These ideas had been continuing to plague her since they were first released. Re-writing all of her works is a huge undertaking, but she hopes her readers will love the new journeys she can take them on now and into the future. Medusa's Curse is the first of the re-written books to be republished. And she hopes you loved it as much as she loved writing it.

If you would like to keep up to date on her new releases or what new books, she will have coming out next follow her here:

https://linktr.ee/JosslynLeach

ALSO BY JOSSLYN LEACH

HEADLESS BEAUTY

Death Rider Series

Book 1

By Josslyn Leach

CHAPTER 1
HEADLESS BEAUTY

AISLYNN

The pounding of the horse's feet are all I can hear over my thundering heart. I can't even spare a look over my shoulder. I need to make it to the bridge. I'll be safe once I'm across it.

"Come Ais, you can make it." I chide myself as I push myself to run as fast as I can in this God forsaken dress. The branches from trees have torn at it and my hair has fallen out of the pinned hairstyle I had. Now my long red curls are flying wild in the wind. While the rest of the world holds its breath waiting to watch what happens. Will the man on his horse catch me or will I make it across the Silver Hollow Bridge to safety. I should have known better than to walk home alone. That's always when he appears when I'm alone.

Normally he watches from the shadows.

Tonight, though is different, the moon is red as blood and the night dark even with its giant presence lighting up the sky.

The cool breeze hitting my skin makes me feel like death is near.

I smile triumphantly as the bridge is less than 10 feet away. With being so close to safety I chance a look behind me. Shocked to find the mystery man and his horse having disappeared.

I stop in place. Looking around to see if he moved off path. But he is gone.

I'm safe.

Smiling to myself as I feel like I have won this battle with death.

I then turn around running right into a dark figure.

"I'm sorry." His deep voice says before he swings his golden scathe with an hourglass sitting on the top.

As I close my eyes, I feel no pain.

Shooting up in bed, my eyes frantically search around the room while I'm panting worse than Ash, my Pegasus after I make him run.

He prefers flying and gladly reminds me every day.

After a few moments of time my heart drops to my normal steady beat, I look over at the clock to see its only 2 am.

Why me, I've been plagued with nightmares for weeks now. It's not fair. Why can't I dream happy dreams? Or no dreams.

I could get down with a dreamless sleep.

Giving up on sleep, I head over to my window seat, my book from earlier still sitting were I left it only a few hours earlier.

Picking up the book I settle down on the amongst my hundreds of pillows I have place on this thing and top off my measure of comfort with a sage green knitted blanket.

Once I'm all sorts of comfortable and talk myself out of

wanting tea to, I open the book to the page I left off and dive back into the world that isn't my own.

This is my perfect heaven and the claim moment I needed before I leave for Silver Hollow College.

Located in the Findara the central of all our lands. Its where the fates rule from as they run the college that allows them to make sure each future ruler and others are still fit for their destiny.

I'm amongst one of those others. As the daughter of the Headless Horseman, while my mother one of the last of her kind an angel of death. She told me once there were thousands like us for all different purposes, but a great war broke out and now only less a hundred are still alive.

I was definitely another with that parental mixture with gifts that not even my parents knew I'd have. So, after my mother had me, they moved to Cosmotellurian the only island that isn't sectioned for specific species aside from Findara.

And now for the first time ever I am leaving my home for the first time, to learn more about my gifts and hopefully return with a purpose.

One thing is for sure I'm glad I'll have my best friend Piper with me on this new adventure.

"Aislynn, you need to get up its almost time for you to leave." I hear my mother say from the other side of my bedroom door.

Which of course scares the living day crap out of me causing me to fall off the window seat that I must have finally fell back to sleep on.

"You okay Aisly?" My mother asks while trying to hold back a laugh.

"Just peachy." I reply as untangle myself from my blanket and stand up.

"Good get dressed and meet us downstairs." she adds before walking back out the room before I can say anything else.

Heading to my bathroom I jump in the shower washing up really quickly, my stomach is swarming with butterfly's. I'm nervous about what I'll have to face going to Silver Hollow.

Most of the others are same species rarely do others mate outside of their own kind, yet here I am proof they can.

Lacing up my boots I check out myself in the mirror smiling, my long red hair I left down in natural waves while my makeup is set to perfection. I decided on a long green riding jacket with silver buttons.

The smell of coffee and bacon comes from outside my door. My mother's special way of calling me down to eat.

Taking one last look at my room I head downstairs for the last time till winter break.

"There is my darling daughter," My father says while pulling me into a hug.

I chuckle, "been getting into the fae wine again dad?" I ask as I look up at him raising my eyebrow in question.

"I told you not to be weird Theo, now she is going to rush right out that door without eating if you keep this up." my mother chastises my dad while handing me a mug full of coffee.

"He's not the only weird one." I say as I take my precious cup over to the table.

I take my seat in my spot while my parents sit down, we all load up our plates with food.

"Do you have everything you need for school?" my mother asks again, even after we packed up everything a few days ago and sent it off to the school yesterday along with Ash my familiar.

"I believe so." I reply before shoving a bite of my waffle into my mouth.

I'll miss my mother's cooking, though thankfully my parents informed me there was a student cafeteria. This girl and cooking are not a good combo, I get to easily distracted and forget about the food till it's burned to a crisp and smelling up the place.

"If not, we can send it to you, just let us know of your mirror." my father adds in before we all fall into a silence company while we eat.

Once we finish eating, we clean up together, my parents talking about their found memories at Silver Hollow. Telling me how they met there, a story I've heard my whole life but never get tired of hearing.

It's a love story that most others dream of my parents were true mates. It's very rare for another to find their true mate. No one is truly sure as to why, I have my own theories, but I'll never know if they are true.

"It's time to go Aislynn," my mother says to me. I nod as we make our way out to our stables, I wish Ash was still here so I could ride him over to the portal in the center of town.

To keep everything organized each student and their family has a certain time to arrive at the portal all of our things and familiars if we have one are taken the day before. I guess it makes the process a lot faster.

"Aislynn Vortez, you have five minutes to say goodbye and step through the portal." Agar the portal mage tells me.

I nod my understanding to him before I face my parents, "I'll call you as soon as I can." I tell them.

"Be safe." my mother says, "and try to experience everything you can."

"I will." I promise her before my father is pulling me from her hold into his arms.

"Don't forget your head, and kick ass if you need to."

"I always do." I remind him.

"I know you do my little pumpkin. Now go find your adventure."

Nodding I pull aways from my parents and with my head held high I walk to the portal, looking back once I wave at my parents before I step through.